I0662695

Bone
of My Bones

by

Debra Doggett

Bone of My Bones

Cover Art by *Debbie Taylor*

The Wild Rose Press, Inc.
PO Box 708
Adams Basin, NY 14410-0708
Visit us at www.thewildrosepress.com

Publishing History
First Black Rose Edition, 2015
Print ISBN 978-1-5092-0281-2
Digital ISBN 978-1-5092-0282-9

Published in the United States of America

There was something about the etched design in the faded cowhide, sort of a scripted "E" all fancied up, that looked all too familiar.

"Hey, those are Eddie's boots. Whoa!" With the aid of the side of the house, Leon got to his feet and peered at me with bloodshot eyes.

"What?" I kicked at the dirt with my slipper, trying to push enough of it aside to get a better view.

"You bumped him off."

"What are you babbling about?" I shined the light around the edge of the hole Leon had dug. They really did look like Eddie's boots. Please, please, please, don't let the rest of him be in them.

"You bumped Eddie off, didn't you?"

Leon staggered against me, giving me a good whiff of his breath. I wondered if you could get drunk from secondhand alcohol. Right now I could really use a stiff drink. I gripped his arm to keep him still. His wavering combined with his breath nauseated me. He peered into my eyes then looked back down at the ground.

"I mean, you always said you wanted to but I never really thought you would." His voice held the kind of awe he usually reserved for major sports events and winners of monster truck rallies. It was the most respect he'd ever given my work.

I shook my head and hissed at him. "I did not bump Eddie off. You don't know this is Eddie. It could be a total stranger."

"You bumped off a total stranger?" The awe factor faltered a bit, replaced by a note of fear.

Dedication

For Kate, Lori, Tori, Tracy, Jess, Janie,
Wendy, Mark, Jake, Rebecca, Sherrie,
and the Order of the Cauldron of the Sage.
Thanks for all you taught me.

Chapter One

Solving Eddie's murder might be doable, even for an amateur like me. It would only take finding the particular person he'd pissed off this time. Explaining why he was buried in my front yard might be more difficult.

After my first horrified thought flashed through my mind, as I shined the flashlight down at his feet, I had a second, more selfish one. *Shit, I divorced him five years ago, and he's still messing up my life.* Unkind I know, but Eddie never visited unless he brought trouble along. I had to admit, though, this was a stretch even for him. And the sad part, I couldn't blame it only on Eddie. As big a fool as he was, he couldn't have planted himself under my prized roses on his own.

I could, however, blame my idiotic little brother, Leon, for bringing Eddie's latest visit to my attention. If he hadn't fallen into my roses while stumbling home from another night of mindless drinking, he might have made it to the front door, and we'd have been none the wiser. Instead, a misstep landed him right in the middle of the thorn-covered bushes. He ripped two of them out of the dirt while rolling around in pain. That's how he uncovered Eddie's feet.

"What the hell's that? Hey, those look like old boots. Who'd bury old boots in the front yard?"

"I don't know, Leon. Why do you have to do this?

You're driving me crazy, and it's hell on my roses." I tugged on his arm, sliding him forward across the broken branches.

"Don't start your bitching. After all, what's more important, your only brother or these damn roses?"

"The roses." I had him almost to his feet when he plopped back down and jerked his arm away.

"That is cold, Rose, really cold. I'm a man with a broken heart. I deserve some sympathy."

"You're a man with a drinking problem, and you deserve a kick in the ass."

"A broken heart, Rose. Did you hear me? I've been abandoned, betrayed, dumped, used and abused…"

Leon had been singing this tune since he lost his job, his girlfriend and his sobriety, and I lost my sanity long enough to let him move back in with me. I ignored the rest of his rant and focused my attention on getting him to his feet. I'd almost accomplished it when he leaned over again and braced himself against the dirt.

"Hey, I'm telling you, there's something buried here." He started to dig in the soft soil.

"Stop it, Leon, that's a Golden Prize canary yellow antique rose. Don't be digging it up, or you'll kill it."

"Yeah, well then you could grow catnip and crap like that, like you're supposed to."

"Catnip is for cats, why would I grow that? I don't have a cat."

"Because you don't listen to me. Witches are supposed to own a cat that, you know, follows them around and creeps everybody out."

"It's not a hard and fast rule. And I'm allergic to cat hair, remember? Besides, why would I want to creep everybody out? My spells are supposed to help them."

"You gotta have mystique, Rosie."

I ducked just in time to miss the clump of dirt he tossed over his shoulder.

"Otherwise folks won't put any stock in those stupid spells of yours." He jerked his arm back and pulled another branch off my rosebush. He used it to help himself to his knees. "Even your sign is dull. Where's the mystery in saying Rosalie DeSalvo, witch for hire, huh? No wonder you don't ever get to do the good stuff."

I resisted the urge to shove his face back into my beloved rosebushes, more for their sake than his. Instead I struggled to get him standing, my words puffing out with the effort.

"I am not about to argue business sense and marketing with a drunk. And keep your comments about my sign to yourself. I get enough flak from Aunt Anya over it."

"I thought that was why you put it up, to get under her skin."

That part might have some truth to it. My Aunt Anya was a devout Catholic. We'd never been close. Every family dinner, every holiday event, hell, every Sunday she'd find another way to ask me why I didn't just join one of those witch groups and do my crazy stuff in some secret meeting under the cover of darkness instead of out in the open where God and everyone could see. If I wanted to go to Hell in a hand basket there was no reason why I should tarnish the family name in the process. I tried to tell her that being different was what New Mexico was all about, which in most parts of the state would be true. But we were up in the northwest corner, and God alone ruled here. None of that crazy New Age shit was to be tolerated in guns and oil country. Leave that for the wackos and the tourists in Santa Fe.

So maybe my sign did have more than one point to it, although I stuck to my story that my path had nothing to do with my family. I'd chosen to be a solitary witch because the truth was I didn't play well with others. Leon said the real problem was that others didn't want to play with me, but brothers are often cruel, and sisters should never pay any attention to what they say. At least not for the first thirty years of their relationship. Leon still had six years to go before anything he said carried any weight. Unlike his body, which at the moment carried more weight than I wanted to lift. Just as I had him standing semi-erect, he tilted to one side and, for a moment, I thought he was going to be sick.

"You better not puke on my roses."

"I ain't gonna puke on your stupid bushes." He braced both hands against the side of the house to steady himself. Then he giggled. "But you'd have to thank me if I did 'cause it'd be fertilizer for them."

"You're disgusting."

He started to slide sideways, and I caught his arm. His voice held the effects of another night spent on a barstool. "I think I need to get inside."

"I think you need to get a grip," I mumbled. "I could be nice and comfy on the couch. Or better yet, in bed. Instead I'm out here picking you up out of the dirt."

"I'm telling you, I think I'm gonna be sick after all."

"Then you better think about standing up. If I have to drag your drunk ass into the house the least you could do is help." Leon let out a moan that turned into a retching sound, and I shook my head. "For that matter, if you're going to drink yourself into a stupor every night, why don't you just do it at home, where you're on the couch to start with. You could at least save me that much trouble."

"Why you got to bitch about everything I do?"

"Everything? You say that like there's some diversity involved. This is it, Leon, this is all you do. Drink. I'm tired, and I want to be in bed. That's where normal people are at this hour."

"Well that lets you out, then."

I went to smack him, but he leaned all the way over before I could connect.

"Whoa, I need to sit down."

Before I could protest or drag him back up, Leon plopped down on the ground, managing to mangle yet another of my precious roses. He tilted to one side, and I thought he might puke after all, a sound I really didn't want to hear. Instead he peered down at the dirt like he'd lost something.

"They really are boots." He smirked up at me. "Maybe you got some mystique after all. You got a body down here, too? What happened, Rose, did you send one of them spells of yours to somebody, and it didn't work, as usual, so you planted 'em in the front yard when they croaked?"

I kicked at him, but he slumped against the house laughing, and I missed. I contented myself with glaring, even though in the dark it didn't have quite the same effect.

"It's *cast*, not *send*. You cast spells, Leon, you don't mail them to people. And my spells don't always go bad."

He kept chuckling as he leaned over again, digging in the dirt he'd upended from the flower bed. This time my kick connected, but all I got for the effort was a grunt. True, as a general rule, my spells don't pan out to their full potential. That was Alexis' diplomatic way of putting it. Alexis Delacourte, High Priestess of the local coven, had agreed to mentor me three years ago, but I think she'd like to find a way out of the commitment if she could. That seems to be the story of my life. Full of people who don't want to commit. I will admit I have some trouble with the advanced techniques of the Craft. But I had the basics down. I've come a long way. Even Alexis said so. Grudgingly.

"Besides." I glowered at Leon, who was tossing dirt to each side like he was uncovering hidden gold. "Why would I dig up my own roses to bury somebody under them? Granny Claire gave me those roses on my thirteenth birthday. They're special."

Leon ignored me. I knelt closer to the ground to see what he was busy digging around. As I went down, he came up, and we met in the middle with a thud.

"Ow, why'd you hit me, Rose?"

"I don't know, Leon, you just bring out the violent side of me." I rubbed my forehead and sighed. "Get out of the way so I can see what that is."

"I told you, it's boots." He frowned. "Boots with somebody's feet in them."

I focused the tiny beam from the flashlight at the battered boots sticking out of the soft ground of my flowerbed then had a sinking feeling. There was something about the etched design in the faded cowhide, sort of a scripted "E" all fancied up, that looked all too familiar.

"Hey, those are Eddie's boots. Whoa!" With the aid of the side of the house, Leon got to his feet and peered at me with bloodshot eyes.

"What?" I kicked at the dirt with my slipper, trying to push enough of it aside to get a better view.

"You bumped him off."

"What are you babbling about?" I shined the light around the edge of the hole Leon had dug. They really did look like Eddie's boots. *Please, please, please, don't let the rest of him be in them.*

"You bumped Eddie off, didn't you?"

Leon staggered against me, giving me a good whiff of his breath. I wondered if you could get drunk from secondhand alcohol. Right now I could really use a stiff drink. I gripped his arm to keep him still. His wavering combined with his breath nauseated me. He peered into my eyes then looked back down at the ground.

"I mean, you always said you wanted to but I never really thought you would." His voice held the kind of awe he usually reserved for major sports events and winners of monster truck rallies. It was the most respect he'd ever given my work.

I shook my head and hissed at him. "I did not bump Eddie off. You don't know this is Eddie. It could be a total stranger."

"You bumped off a total stranger?" The awe factor faltered a bit, replaced by a note of fear.

"Leon, go in the house before I bump you off." I let go of his arm, and Leon pitched downward. Against my better judgment, I caught him before he hit the ground.

After I got Leon into the house and onto the couch, I found him a pair of tweezers to pick out the thorns, then got the shovel and the flashlight and headed back outside. Fear warred with the pain gathering around my heart as I stared down at the pile of dirt that might contain the remains of my ex-husband. A dark feeling warned me I didn't want to do this, didn't want to see this. And I didn't want the neighbors to see it. So, I ignored the warning.

Thinking of the neighbors made me grateful, yet again, that my little house stood at the end of a gravel road and faced the Animas River. Not that I usually did strange things during the night, or at least not before Leon had come back to stay. I had told the Universe I was open to new things. Guess it was taking me up on it. It probably didn't get much stranger than digging your ex-husband up out of the flowerbed.

Thoughts of how he'd gotten in the flowerbed decided to rear their scary heads as I struck another shovelful of dirt. I hadn't noticed anything weird when I came home, but it was already dark by then. I didn't make a habit of checking out my roses every time I came home. The thought of some killer coming by my house and taking the time to bury a dead body there made me rethink my *naiveté* about the world I lived in. Granted, one reason I'd let Leon move in was because I thought it would be safer having someone else living here. That belief stemmed partly from my aunt's incessant harping about how it was unsafe for a woman to live alone. Guess an alcoholic who spent his nights on a barstool didn't really change that. Leon was never going to qualify for security guard of the year in his present state.

Deciding those thoughts weren't much better than the previous ones, I pushed them away and looked back down at the problem. Sucking up my courage, I rammed the shovel into the soft dirt, cringing at the thud it made. I closed my eyes and thought of other things to keep my mind off what lay under all that dirt. I thought of police cars screaming into my driveway, of handcuffs, body cavity searches and a long prison sentence. Then I remembered every time I'd threatened Eddie with death and dismemberment. And all the folks who'd heard my threats. I could see Aunt Anya, sobbing into a handkerchief on the witness stand as she lamented the fact I'd fallen into the trap of evil just like she'd always said would happen. Yep, it would be prison for me, Eddie's ultimate act of destruction in my life. All the old anger surfaced again. Then I got a look at Eddie's face.

I don't know what I'd expected. Maybe the peaceful look of sleep I'd seen on my daddy's face as he lay in his silver coffin. Eddie might be dead, but the look on his face told me it hadn't been peaceful. Or the look on what was left of his face. I dropped to my knees and puked all over my roses. Along with making me lose my supper, the sight in front of me broke what was left of my hard feelings toward Eddie into little pieces. Nobody should die like that.

Once I had Eddie above ground, I found an old tarp and pulled him to my greenhouse around back. I only had to stop to puke one more time. Not the best night I'd had this week. With Eddie out of view, I headed for the phone then remembered Alexis left last Wednesday for a Wicca gathering in Mexico. Another reason I liked the solitary craft. Having that many witches in one place sounded like power overload to me.

So I put in an emergency call to the only one I knew who'd still be awake at this time. Mama Toulouse had wandered into the desert forty years ago from Port Arthur, Louisiana, looking for a wider and more mystical arena for her magickal talents. For reasons known only to her spirit guide, she had stopped in the only ultraconservative, Bible-Belt region of the entire southwest United States. She liked to say it was her purpose in life to bring a breath of diversity to this world.

Past seventy now, she spent mornings watching her favorite soaps and afternoons and evenings telling fortunes and giving advice. For as long as I could remember, she had been my Granny Claire's friend. Since neither of my parents had any interest in the Craft, Mama appointed herself my magickal guardian after Granny Claire's death. The truth was Mama wasn't much better at predicting than I was at spells. Still, I needed a certain kind of help tonight and, hey, any port in a storm. My chosen port took five rings to answer her phone. I was beginning to worry I might be in the storm all alone when she finally picked up.

"Who the hell is this calling me at this fucking time of the night? This better be a real fucking emergency or I'm gonna send a spell through this phone that'll cut off your vital parts and do all kinda nasty shit to…"

Okay, so maybe I was wrong about her being awake. I held the phone away from my ear through the rest of her tirade. I was pretty sure some of the threats she made couldn't happen to me since I didn't have the right anatomy for them. One could never tell with Mama though. I didn't hang up. She was the closest thing to the kind of help I needed.

"Mama, it's Rose. I need your help."

"Rose? What the hell you doing up this time of night? Ain't you got nothing better to do than to be wandering around in the dark? Shit, girl, staying up all the time won't make your spells any better. You need to be getting a good night's sleep."

I sensed one of her lectures in the making. If I didn't stop it now, she wouldn't take a breath for at least another ten minutes, and I had no time to waste.

"Mama, it's an emergency. I need you to come over as fast as you can."

"Come over? It's the middle of the night. What, you think I walk around my house dressed to go visiting? I got my gown on. An emergency?"

"Yes. Please, Mama, get here quick, preferably before sunrise."

Since the drive from her house to mine took less than fifteen minutes, and it was a good four hours or more till sunrise, I considered the time frame generous.

"Before sunrise? What the hell kind of emergency you got?"

"A big one." I hung up the phone before she could answer.

I'd worked my body into a wringing sweat and my nerves into a near frenzy by the time I heard Mama's ancient Rambler coming down the road. For most of the half hour it had taken her to get here, I'd created scenario after scenario of what might happen to me because of Eddie's latest visit. None of them were comforting, and all but one involved me doing jail time. The other involved me living out of the back of my pickup for the rest of my life, working odd jobs and

11

moving in the dead of night every month or so.

As Mama eased her six-foot frame out of the car, a part of me breathed a sigh of relief when I saw she was in full regalia. It was an impressive sight, a mix of magick and know-how meant to dazzle. Mama took her chosen calling to heart. No one could accuse her of not dressing the part. Twenty-six years of working for K-Mart gave her a strong belief in marketing and an unwavering commitment to sparing no expense when it came to work clothes. It was all part of the game, she said. And the game was meant to be won. I had to admire her efforts. From the orange and purple turban that covered her cropped gray frizz to the hem of the paisley caftan that flowed over her bulk, the casual observer would think she oozed magick as she walked. Her outfit told me she took my emergency pretty serious, a small reassurance I found I needed. I just hoped it would be enough. As I waved her back to the storage shed, I could only regret that looks aren't everything.

Chapter Two

"Damn, and he was such a good-looking son of a bitch."

Mama stared down at the tarp Eddie lay on. Or what was left of him. Someone had sliced his face to ribbons, continuing the hatchet job down most of his chest and ending with one long, violent slash across his throat. It was a brutal sight. Whomever Eddie pissed off this time, they took it out all over him and then some. He looked like an after-battle Viking sacrifice lying there among the rows of flowers and herbs that lined the wooden shelves of the greenhouse. Only for his funeral it would be me doing the burning if I couldn't figure out what had happened to him.

"Damn, damn, damn. Look at that poor boy. He used to be such a pretty thing walking around like he owned the town." Mama shook her head. "My, my, my."

Goddess knows that was the truth. Eddie had been quite a sight strutting down the streets of Aztec, a sight plenty of girls couldn't take their eyes off, me included. Eddie strutted my way, and my brain exited stage left. At first, that seemed okay. Eddie was a physical kind of guy. Later I'd realize how little his good looks counted when it came to marriage. I shook my head to clear out the past and tend to the present.

"Mama, I need you to focus for a minute. I am in

deep shit here. I've got a rapidly decomposing ex-spouse lying in my greenhouse and a major migraine threatening to blow the top of my head off. Can't you think of anybody who can help me out of this?"

"Child, you need to call the undertaker. You got to bury this boy."

I squeezed my eyes shut and counted to ten, hoping by the time I opened them again I could make my voice at least pretend to be calm. "Mama, you can't just drop off people to the undertaker to bury. They tend to want a little information, and other important stuff, like a death certificate, for instance. I don't think they'd understand if I said hi, I'm Rosalie DeSalvo, the crazy witch lady who lives out County Road 450, and I found this guy buried in my front yard, so could you bury him somewhere else for me. He's messing up my roses. What's that? Oh, his name? Well, it's Eddie DeSalvo. He's my ex-husband. And he's not going back under my roses."

"You need to go to the police and tell 'em you divorced him years ago, and you don't want him hanging around no more."

I bit the inside of my mouth. It stung, but a little pain seemed safer right at the moment than saying what came to mind. Leon stumbled into the doorway.

"You could stick him in a vat of lime. That'll eat away all his flesh. He'll be nothing but dry bones then. We could—"

"Shut up, Leon. Mama, I can't go to the police. It would be the same problem as the undertaker. I've got to get Eddie away from here, away from me. Don't you know some kind of revealing spell that would show us what happened to him or better yet, some spell that would make him disappear?"

"Somebody sliced the shit outta him, that's what happened to him."

"Shut up, Leon." I rubbed my hands over my forehead, massaging at the tension that pounded there. "Mama, think. I mean, if we can find out who did this, if I can solve his murder…"

I swallowed hard as I said it. Even though I'd threatened him with it often enough, the sight of Eddie lying there bloody and still brought a whole new meaning to my threats.

"If I can find out who did it, who…killed him, then maybe I can get the police to believe me and not haul *me* off to jail. I don't want to go to prison. Divorce was supposed to have taken care of getting Eddie out of my life. After all I went through, I shouldn't have to spend the next fifty years in prison for his murder. Can't you think of something we can do?" I heard the edge of hysteria in my voice and took a couple of deep breaths.

"We?" Mama shifted backward, edging toward the door until she bumped into Leon.

"What about that coven over in Bloomfield? Would any of them know some spell we could use?"

"Use to do what?" Mama shook her head with enough vigor to have her threaded bone earrings rattling. "This poor thing here can't tell you nothing anymore." Mama frowned down at Eddie. "This boy's dead." She leaned down closer and stared. "All the way dead. Somebody sure made a mess of that pretty face. Don't know what you can do about it now."

"There's got to be something." I paced a circle around the tarp, trying hard to ignore the body in the middle of it. The scent of the flowers was starting to make me a bit queasy. "There's just got to be something."

"Why don't you take him and bury him out in the desert? Let him get mummified out there and then some archaeologist can dig him up later. He could be a really big deal, they could maybe call him Slash Man and write a bunch of articles wondering why he had MacDonald's fries in his stomach when he's a thousand-year-old mummy. There's lots of room out there. You could put him anywhere. It'd be years before they found him. I say haul him off. That way you get him away from here."

Drunks are no help in a crisis. I glared at Leon. "Now why didn't I think of that, little brother? I could just throw him in the back of the pickup and drive around till I find a really good spot. Hell, it's going to be daylight soon, maybe we can ask the neighbors to help us get him in the truck."

Leon smiled and opened his mouth, and I gritted my teeth, fully expecting him to offer to go and knock on Mrs. Carvey's door and ask her for a shovel. Mama interrupted him.

"Well, maybe we don't have to throw out that whole thought with the bathwater."

"What?" I stopped pacing long enough to stare at her.

"Could be you could find somebody else to take him off."

"I'll get the yellow pages."

Mama gave me a blank stare as my sarcasm flew over her head. She tapped a finger on her chin then smiled.

"Well, now, I heard tell of a nest of vampires out

on old Lightner Road. They could take him in, make him one of their own."

I rubbed my hands over my face again and tried not to scream. Crawling back in my bed and forcing the police to pry me out of it was sounding better and better.

"Mama, as you pointed out, Eddie's already dead."

"Well, so are they." She gave me a patient look, like she was waiting for the pitiful child to catch on.

I held my tongue. It was getting harder, but I refused to snap under pressure. Maybe later. I'd owe it to myself later.

"Yes, but they didn't get really dead. Well, they did but it's…different. Eddie's completely dead. Stone-cold dead. All the way dead. And has been for a while."

I stared back down at the tarp and shuddered as I forced myself not to think about what had been done to Eddie. "Besides, dead people don't just turn into vampires. In the first place, they've got to be bitten, not sliced to pieces. There's a way it happens; they've got to be bitten by a vampire, and it's a certain kind of bite, and then they die for three days only they don't really die, they just lose their soul. Mama, don't you know how any of this happens?"

"'Course I know how it happens," she snapped. "I ain't stupid. I been doing this shit longer than you have, years longer. I just don't think well under pressure."

"We could dig a big…"

"Leon, don't talk to me again until you're sober. Go into the house and lay down on the couch, or there'll be a spell waiting for you in the mail today. A bad one."

"All of yours are bad ones."

"Leon, I'm not gonna warn you again. You weren't my idea. I never wanted a brother in the first place. You were supposed to be Mary Kathleen." I took a step toward him, and he held up both hands.

"Okay, okay. Geez, try to help and that's the thanks you get. Fine, do it your stupid witch way. That's all you think about."

He stomped past Mama, who nudged Eddie with her toe.

"He is all the way dead, ain't he?"

"All the way. Probably the first thing outside of sex Eddie's finished doing since 1998."

Mama tapped a finger on her chin. "You know, I don't mess around in that dark shit, but…" She cleared her throat a few times.

"But what?" I closed my eyes, wondering if I really wanted to hear her next suggestion.

"But maybe there is a way."

I glanced over at her, and she wouldn't meet my gaze. Not a good sign.

"A way to? Mama, don't make me work any harder. I'm not up to it. A way to what?"

"A way to find out what it is you want to know. There is a guy lives out this side of Fruitland. I don't know him personal, but I've heard things."

"Things? What things?"

"That he can do things. Things that might be what you're looking for, that might get you what you need. That might make your little problem disappear."

My little problem? "He makes people disappear? What is he, the mafia?"

She snorted. "Ain't no mafia out here. All we got is them weird ass Mexican gang wannabes. No, this guy

18

brings people back."

"I thought you said he made them disappear."

"I said he could make your problem disappear."

"By bringing it back? Bringing it back from where?"

"From the dead."

"From the dead? Mama, are you saying this guy's a necromancer?"

"I don't know. Told you I didn't know him personal. Don't have no way of knowing what he does on his own time. But for business he raises people from the dead."

I had a niggling moment of pure selfishness as I considered her words. Having Eddie dead wasn't what I had issues with. Granted, I wouldn't have wished the kind of suffering he'd gone through on him. My wishes had included more of the emotional and verbal torture. Still, so long as he was buried elsewhere, I could get used to his passing. A few tears, a little public grieving and he'd be part of my past with no future trouble in sight. *Why, oh why couldn't anything in my life be simple?*

"I just want to find out who killed Eddie and dumped him here." I shook my head. "I don't want him back."

"It's not like you're gonna keep him." Mama's gaze met mine, and there was sympathy in it. "Hell, you didn't keep him when he was living. He'll go away again. But what better way to find out what you need to know than to ask Eddie himself? He oughta know who killed him."

I had to admit she had a point. But I knew Eddie. Just because he was supposed to know something didn't mean he would. I stared down at him. Damn, he had been a good-looking son of a bitch. Somebody sure fixed that. So did I really want him up and around, able to open his mouth again? After all, talking wasn't his strong point and with his looks gone…what the hell, I didn't have any other options. I backed away from the tarp and took a deep breath. *Was I really crazy enough, or desperate enough to do this?*

"How much money?"

"His fee? Don't know. Ain't never heard nobody talk about that. Could probably find his address, you could go ask him."

"And leave Eddie here on his own? Not on a bet. Can you get me his phone number?"

"Probably. Naomi should have it. She dabbles every once in a while in that dark shit. Fix me some eggs, and I'll give her a call."

I nodded, hoping my stomach was up to scrambled eggs. As I pulled the tarp over Eddie, I whispered to him. "You better know who did it, you bastard. 'Cause if you don't, I'll kill you again myself. And this time you're going under the compost heap."

Chapter Three

I'd paced back and forth so much since hanging up the phone Leon went into the bedroom saying I was giving him motion sickness. Maybe I was only passing on the nausea I got after the scrambled eggs. Mama had called her friend Naomi to get the number for Mr. M. Romero, and I'd made the call, for all the good it did my nerves. Nothing about the sound of the cold voice on the other end of the line comforted me. Nor did anything he said, which was damn little. He was terse and to the point, asking few questions and taking a long pause before agreeing to come to the house. The drive would take him about thirty minutes. I was at twenty-eight minutes and pacing.

"Would you sit down or something, else I'm going to have to go in the bedroom with Leon and Lord knows he's not gonna like that." Mama stretched her legs out on my tiny couch, settling back against the flowered pillows I'd made in high school Home Economics class.

"I can't. Are you sure about this guy, Mama? He's not going to come in and do something I'll regret, is he?"

"Something like bringing Eddie back from the dead?"

"Wait a minute, that was your idea. Now you think it's a bad one?"

"Oh, quit your worrying." She glanced over at me with that look in her eye that always made me nervous. "You oughta go in your room and spruce up a bit before he comes. It'll make you feel better. Naomi says he's single."

"I'm not asking him to take me to the movies, Mama. I want the man to revive my dead ex-husband, not my sex life. Besides, it's three o'clock in the morning. Nobody's supposed to look good at this time."

"Man can do more than one thing if you give him a reason. Might make you feel a little better to do a bit of fixing up before you talk to him."

"What'll make me feel better is to get Eddie out of my greenhouse and back in the ground. Somebody else's ground."

Mama played with the remote while I paced some more. I didn't get much TV reception this far out, which didn't bother me but was a source of deep discontent for Leon. Guess Mama felt the same way. She made the entire circle of available channels about three times before tossing the remote to the floor in disgust as she mumbled something about my lack of cable. I stopped and stared out the window. Twenty-nine minutes and counting.

"So you really think I should go and put on a dress?"

She looked me up and down then frowned. "No, better stick with slacks. Dresses aren't always kind, and short women got to watch out for certain fashion issues. Even four or five pounds can show in some clothes."

"I'm not short. I'm average height."

"You on the short end of average, then." She held up a hand as I started to protest. "And that quarter inch you're always trying to stick on to it don't help. Five four is five four. People sizes round up or down, just like dress sizes. You go to the rack at J.C. Penney's, and they got size tens, then you go up a whole number, take 'em or leave 'em. There aren't no size 10 and a half. Hell, most places they don't even give you an 11. They know the truth of things. If you're trying to squeeze your ass into a size 10 and can't, then you're probably not going to be able to get it into a 10 and a half either. Best to move on up. Rounding, that's what the world believes in. So, that quarter inch don't get you anywhere but right back down to five four."

"Five four isn't all that short. It's really more like average," I mumbled. "And I wear a size 8, thank you very much." I went back to pacing.

"And that hair of yours is…"

"Don't start on my hair. You're not giving me another perm. Ever." I gripped my brown locks with both hands. I'd made them a promise of protection after the last time I'd given in. My hair had stuck straight out at an almost perfect ninety-degree angle for two months after Mama persuaded me into letting her give me "just a curl or two".

"Okay, okay, let the whole mess hang straight as string beans then." She folded her arms across her massive bosom as she muttered under her breath. "Like a curl or two would kill you. Few highlights, a little red in that sand brown, and you just might see another date before you get too old to remember how it works."

"How what works?" Leon's comment was muffled by the food he was shoving in his mouth as he stood in the doorway.

"Nothing." I glared at him. "And stop getting

crumbs on the floor. I swept already."

He mumbled something about bitchy women before ambling back to his room, leaving a trail of crumbs down the hall.

The sound of tires on gravel kept me from having to move my pacing outside to avoid Mama's grumbling. Betting on a more positive energy flow than I'd had so far, I told myself my savior had arrived. It was about time I got more saviors and fewer burdens landing on my doorstep. I'm all about the visualization thing.

The porch light illuminated the front yard, making the house look like a welcoming beacon against the dark night. I peeked through the curtains to get a glimpse of him so I could prepare myself.

It didn't take more than a glance to know there was no way I was prepared for this. He didn't just get out of the sleek little sports car, he flowed out of it, like he was part of the darkness around him. That could have been my imagination working overtime. Or not. After all, dark angels can fly, can't they?

A second glance told me I might have more trouble tonight than a dead ex-husband. The man standing in my front yard made me revise my opinion of nobody looking good this early. Something told me this guy looked good 24/7. Just like dark angels are supposed to look so they can lure in the unsuspecting and unprepared innocents they desire to devour. I'd spent three months with Alexis learning to read auras, and this guy's was coming through loud and clear.

He was neither on the short end or average. As a matter of fact, on my somewhat limited experience meter, he went way above average. Tall and lean, he stared around him as he got out of the car, giving me a moment to continue inspecting him. The light wasn't enough to show his face. Though he looked toward the house, his features were shrouded in shadows.

Dressed all in black from the tight slacks that outlined muscles that made me go damp in places I'd neglected far too long, to the duster that swirled around his legs as he walked, he moved through the night like he owned it. His dark hair fell long enough to lie on his shoulders, adding to the dangerous picture he made stalking toward my little stucco house. The coat looked expensive enough to let me know a first date with him wouldn't involve fast food, and the predatory stride told me said date could end in hot sex should he wish it to.

I gulped back the lump that formed in my throat, ready to block any incoherent words I might spit out. I needed to sound sober and sane to this man, not hysterical. I almost giggled at that thought. Who was I kidding? I didn't stand a snowball's chance in Hell of making a good impression. Maybe money would be all he was concerned with. Of course, that just presented another dilemma for me.

"Well?" Mama asked impatiently. "You gonna make me get up and look for myself?"

I motioned to her to quiet down. "Shh, he's coming to the door. We don't want to scare him off."

Mama snorted. "Could you scare him off that easy, he ain't the man you're waiting for. Man does the kind of shit he does shouldn't scare at all, much less easy."

As I watched him stride through the night to my front door, I thought Mama pegged him without even seeing him. Even from behind my flowered curtains, I could tell this man's face held none of the carefree charm Eddie's had. This man walked like someone headed for trouble. Or out to cause some. My positive energy flow started to backpedal, and a whole different set of visuals entered my brain. *What the hell had Eddie gotten me into this time?*

"Are you gonna stand there drooling on the window or open the door for the man?"

I put a finger to my lips to quiet Mama, but she hoisted herself off the couch and headed for the kitchen, grumbling as she went.

"If you ain't gonna dress up, least we can do is offer the man a decent cup of coffee. I'll put the pot on." She ambled into the kitchen.

I thought to tell her it was going to take something stronger than coffee, at least for the two of us. Taking a deep breath, I opened the door before he could knock, hoping it made me look prepared. Then I wished I'd waited.

His expressionless face was a hundred times better looking up close. And a thousand times more dangerous. The dark had hidden a few details that might have kept me from opening the door at all if I'd noticed them. The left side of his face and neck was covered by the intricate design of a tattoo that created the illusion of water and fire swirling together across his deep olive skin. It seemed an unnatural combination, which seemed perfectly natural for the man standing in front of me. There was a small scar above his right eye that looked like someone had carved a small letter C there. Or had tried to. A stubble of dark beard shadowed his face. Guess he hadn't had time to spruce up either.

He stood perfectly still as I stared at him. Nothing on him moved. I wasn't even sure he was breathing. I tried to look somewhere safe, but even his eyes were a dark brown that scared me as much as the rest of him. Something flitting through them reminded me of a restrained tiger, waiting to decide if it was hungry enough to break the leash holding it. I swallowed hard and managed a pleasant smile. *How else did you greet someone who'd come to raise your ex-husband from the dead?*

"Mr. Romero?" A whispered prayer of gratitude went through my head when my voice didn't squeak.

"Expecting somebody else?"

His voice was deep and smooth with a hint of an accent that reverberated inside my head, making me think of an old charm my granny taught me, a spell to hypnotize someone panicky and out of control. *Had I sounded that frantic on the phone?* I needed to pull myself together and quick.

"No," I stammered. "No, you're it. That is if you're Mr. M. Romero."

"Matthias Aloysius Xavier Romero, at your service." He gave me a mock bow, then stood on the steps while I stared at him. "Are you going to let me in or is there some secret test I have to pass first?"

"Oh, I am so sorry." I could hear my nerves doing a tap dance on the base of my skull. So much for first impressions. "Please forgive me, I'm a little frazzled. This has been a very, um, different night for me."

"I would think so."

He brushed past me, and I shivered. The man oozed pheromones. Maybe it was all the leather. And maybe I had gone longer without sex than I remembered for I wanted nothing more than to move up against him again, to rub myself across the muscles covered by that soft black leather. I wasn't usually much for courting danger, so my reaction had me feeling nervous and more than a bit worried. Sort of like the rest of the night had done.

My breath caught in my throat as I watched him moving around my cramped living room, his gaze taking in every detail. I wondered if he had a photographic memory or something because he looked like he was mapping out everything in the room. I also thought it would be scary to be looked at like that, like every secret you possess being sucked out of you by the magick even a lightweight like me could sense playing across his skin. Then he turned those brown eyes my way. Yep, I was right. Scary.

"I'm sure it's not every night you put in an emergency call to someone in my line of work." He made an attempt at a smile. I wondered if it was meant to comfort me or if it was because he realized I was scared shitless. It didn't look like an expression he made very often. "You don't look old enough to have had many ex-husbands end up dead on your doorstep."

"No, no Eddie's the first. Body, that is. Well, the first husband too. Or rather ex-husband."

He looked at me without the smile this time. Guess he'd decided it wasn't worth the effort. I shut the door behind me and leaned against it for support. As his gaze went back to the room, I really started to worry. My first impression told me this man was handsome, smart and self-controlled, all qualities that generally scared the crap out of me anyway, even without the extra scary stuff. But it was the second impression that had me sweating. Granny Claire told me one time that I had power inside me I hadn't even tapped. When I thanked her for the compliment, she gave me a stare that chilled all the way through and told me it wasn't a compliment but a warning. She said power never rested easy untapped, and I'd do best if I found an outlet for it. At the time I'd only nodded and told her I sure would. But I didn't, not understanding at all what she meant. I realized as I stared at Matthias Romero that here was a man who'd found an outlet for the power inside him. It sparked out every pore, fairly shooting out of his dark eyes.

He stepped to the wide bookcases that filled one wall and perused the covers on the shelf, content, I suppose, to wait for me to get to the point. Guess he hadn't been impressed with my idle chatter so far. Startled by how much I wanted to simply stare at him and tongue-tied with nerves that had had a very long night, I didn't say anything, hoping my sidelong glances were at least a bit subtle.

The man moved with the grace of someone confident in his own body. Not really a surprise, considering the body he was in. I'd be confident too. At several inches over six feet, I had to tilt my head back a bit to see all of him. The black leather boots he wore made no sound even on my wood floors, and the coat didn't make a rustle when he moved. The man could've snuck up on anyone, something it would probably be good to remember.

"Do I pass inspection?"

His voice rolled over me like the smooth burn of good whiskey. I jumped, both startled and seduced by the sound of it. Something about his accent lit up my insides with a heat they hadn't felt in a long time. I'd found a guy every now and then who managed to make casual sex fun, but something told me Mr. M. Romero would set fire to the sheets. And possibly to the person he was with. Not that I would ever get the chance to prove that theory. After all, he was here for business. And likely not the kind of business that would make him want to look twice at me. A woman who had ex-husbands turning up in her flowerbed probably didn't pass muster as hot guy dating material.

He hadn't even turned around when he spoke, but now he moved up to face me. Guilty at being caught giving him a once over long enough to be rude, I blushed.

"Sorry. Believe it or not my mama did teach me some manners. She'd be embarrassed to see how I've acted tonight."

"Like you said, it's been quite a different night for you." He cocked his head and stared at me. "From the sounds of things, I'd say you've done okay so far."

"You ain't heard all the noise, then."

Mama's grunt had him turning around. She headed for the couch, coffee cup in hand. "Pot of coffee going, if you want some."

"This is Mama Toulouse. Mama, this is Matthias Romero." I turned to him. "At least, I'm assuming you go by Matthias?"

"Yes." He stepped to the couch and took Mama's hand in his before planting a kiss on it. I thought Mama might swoon. Instead, she patted the spot next to her and waved her hand at me as he sat down.

"Rose, get the man some coffee. He's got a big job to do, don't you, sugar?" I'd have sworn she actually batted her eyes at him. "Don't want the man doing that kind of work without a little caffeine in his system.

He's got to be alert and awake."

Knowing the way Mama made her coffee, one cup and Matthias would be awake till next Christmas. "Would you like some coffee?"

He gave me those brown eyes again. Much more staring at him, and I might swoon.

"Maybe later. Right now we should probably get to the reason you called."

"I guess so."

I sat down in the rocker across from him and tucked my hands under my legs to keep from twisting them together. It was a nervous habit, one of many, and I wanted to at least give the appearance of being cool, calm and collected.

"We didn't get a chance to talk much on the phone. Just the bare bones, so to speak."

Mama groaned, and I winced at my unintentional pun. Matthias just stared. He appeared to have no trouble looking cool, calm and collected, and he wasn't even sitting on his hands.

"You found your ex-husband dead on your lawn."

"Actually, he was buried under the rose bushes out front."

"Buried?"

"Yes. Well, all except his feet. That's how we noticed him. His feet were sticking out of the ground."

"You and Mama Toulouse?"

"Uh, no, me and Leon."

"Leon?"

"Oh, my brother, Leon. He noticed Eddie's boots sticking out of the ground first, and he pointed them out to me."

"You and your brother were out gardening at one

o'clock in the morning?"

"No, oh no, um, Leon doesn't do gardening. He wouldn't touch dirt if he had to, at least not if there was a flower in it. And we don't hang out together these days, as most of his hanging out involves alcohol. Lots of alcohol. Not that I mind a drink now and then, but, I mean, really, Leon has no limits."

Out of the corner of my eye, I saw Mama motioning to me in a kind of frantic zip-your-lip sign. I couldn't help myself, I just kept babbling. She rolled her eyes and gave up as I kept pouring out the words.

"No, I was inside here, watching a movie. *Sleepless in Seattle* one of my favorites. I like to play it over every once in a while, you know, 'cause it's a classic. Well, for women it's a classic. I don't guess guys think it is, you know, 'cause it's really a chick flick and all. Guys don't tend to like that kind of movie, do they? At least not the guys I know. I mean, Eddie hated it."

Matthias cleared his throat, and I bit my tongue.

"I'm babbling, aren't I?"

He nodded. "So you and your brother dug Eddie up from your front yard after you noticed his feet sticking out of the ground."

I had to give the man credit for saying it with a straight face. Cool, calm and collected must be the norm for him. My hands stayed under my legs as I nodded.

"Well, it was mostly me."

Mama snorted.

"Actually, it was all me. I sent Leon into the house because he was in his usual state. He's not much help when he's drunk."

"He ain't much help anytime."

I nodded. "Mama's right, Leon's never really much help."

"So you dug him up alone. And where is Eddie now?"

"He's, um, out back."

"And who else knows about Eddie's arrival in your yard?"

"Nobody, just me, Mama and Leon. Well, and now you."

"And you want to bring Eddie back?"

Something about the way he phrased it brought a brief flashback to mine and Eddie's last marriage counselor, a priest who tried to convince me to take the good with the bad when it came to my marriage. He kept saying I needed to take Eddie back when he faltered on the road of matrimony. Those were his exact words. Like Eddie was a car that stalled out every now and then, and I shouldn't trade him in for a new model. Now those words came back to haunt me. *Did I want Eddie back, for any reason?* I swallowed hard.

"Well, I don't want to keep him. I mean, I want to find out what happened to him and to, you know, return him to the scene of the crime."

"By that I take it Eddie was murdered."

Mama snorted. "That boy was sliced like a Christmas ham waiting to be served."

My stomach flip-flopped. "What Mama means is somebody stabbed him."

"Someone stabbed him."

"Oh, yeah, repeatedly. Eddie must've really pissed off whoever killed him. I'm no expert, but even in my unqualified opinion, I'd say the killer was really angry."

"And you have no idea who would want to kill

Eddie?"

"You mean besides Rose herself?" Leon leaned against the kitchen doorway, a smirk on his face.

"Not funny, Leon." I gave him my meanest look, but on the inside I groaned. If I managed to get out of this fiasco without going to jail, my little brother was going to find new accommodations, preferably in rehab. Out of the corner of my eye, I glanced at Matthias, whose face still held no expression. The intimation that he might be sitting across from a murderer didn't seem to make him sweat. Maybe that meant he hadn't passed judgment yet. Or that he figured I wasn't a threat to him.

"Just trying to help out."

"If that's your idea of help you can go back in the bedroom anytime."

I shouted it at his retreating back, blowing all my attempts to look in any way cool or calm. Leon just waved a hand at me over his shoulder as he strolled back down the hall, no doubt to stumble into his bedroom. The sun was almost up, and God forbid he stay awake during daylight hours even to help his only sibling with a major crisis. Without the rest he might drift off to sleep tonight and fall off his barstool.

"I take it that was your brother." Matthias glanced down the hallway.

"Yeah, although I try not to introduce him as family for obvious reasons." I gave a little laugh. Matthias never blinked as he turned that hard gaze back to me. "I may have said something about wishing Eddie would drop dead on a couple of occasions."

"A couple?" Leon hollered from his room.

"Shut up, Leon." I gave Matthias my best I'm-completely-harmless smile. "It was the divorce. Things got kind of messy and afterward, well, there were some hard feelings. And some harsh things said. I mean, you know how it gets. You say things you don't mean."

Stone had more expression than this man.

"Have you ever been divorced?"

"No."

I laughed again, a tittering sound even I had to admit bordered on hysteria. "Well, take it from me you can say a lot of things you don't mean at a time like that." Beneath my legs, my hands twitched, aching to reach each other so they could do their ritual wringing. "I never really meant I wanted Eddie dead. I was angry, but not like that." The image of Eddie's slashed face floated before me, and I thought I might be sick. "Not like that."

Matthias stood and panic clutched at my throat. *Was he leaving? Was he headed for the nearest police station?* I almost jumped when he reached for my hand, pulling me up out of the chair.

"It's going to be daylight soon." His voice was as smooth as before, calmer than anyone could expect. The man could moonlight as a hypnotist. "Since you're telling me you weren't the one who sliced Eddie up." He led me along behind him toward the door. "Let's go see if we can find out just who else Eddie made mad enough to want him dead."

Chapter Four

Matthias was no chattier on the way outside than he'd been inside. But he kept hold of my hand. Whether it was to keep the possibly murdering ex-wife from grabbing any weapons along the way or not, I didn't care. I needed something else to think about besides where we were going and what we were going to do and the tingle of his flesh against mine helped that thought process just fine.

We were halfway across the yard when he stopped. In the dim circle of the back porch light, I nearly stumbled against him. He gripped my hand tighter. I looked at him, trying to temper my what-the-hell expression. He just stared at me for a long moment.

"How old are you?"

"Excuse me?" *The man finally decides to talk and that's what he asks me?*

"On the phone you said Alexis was mentoring you in the Craft."

"Wouldn't it have been easier to ask how long I'd been studying with her?"

He shrugged. "You want to know something, you need to ask specific questions."

So he wanted to know how old I was? Now that was a loaded question if ever I heard one. The kind a smart man would steer clear of. And Matthias Romero struck me as a smart man. It made me wonder what he really wanted to know, if he had some ulterior motive for asking. I pondered the answer for a minute. Did I lie and tell him I was older, and therefore wiser? Or did I knock off a couple of years so he didn't wonder why the hell I wasn't better at this at my age? Did I go for the hot factor? Was it hotter to be 25 than 30? How old was he?

I compromised and went with the truth, something I wouldn't have to try and remember later.

"I turned twenty-eight last month."

He just nodded. I couldn't tell from the look on his face if he'd gotten what he wanted or not from my answer. Maybe all he wanted was to see if I'd lie to him. Then I felt it, not strong but subtle, a bare ripple around the edges of my thoughts. In a reflex action, I pushed back and the ripple broke.

"You're reading me!"

I stopped and let go of his hand, both angry and astonished. No one had ever put the moves on me in that way before.

"Not anymore. You stopped me. Nice to know you noticed, though."

"Nice to know I noticed? You do something that, that…"

"Rude."

"Yeah, that rude and all you can say is nice to know you noticed?"

"Nice to know you noticed and knew what I was doing." He started walking again. "And that you're capable of doing something about it. That helps."

"*Helps?*" I tried not to screech. "*It helps?*"

He started walking, careful not to touch my hand this time. "Most women get flustered when you ask them their age. It throws them off, makes it a good time to check how sensitive they are."

Was he kidding? He had been rude, but I passed the test. I had a hard time deciding whether to be furious or flattered as I reevaluated my infatuation with Mr. Tall, Dark and Strange.

"Just a heads up, pal, that's a dangerous method to use to find out something." I glared at him, hands on my hips.

He paused and looked back at me. "It's an important something. Most important things have an element of risk to them."

"It's that important to find out how good I am?"

I caught the smirk on his face and winced at my unintended double entendre.

"In my line of work it helps to know if people are what and who they say they are."

"I'll bet," I mumbled.

His answer begged another question, one I wasn't sure how to go about finding the answer to until it was too late for the answer to make a difference. I'd been so focused on getting him to trust me enough to help me, I hadn't considered whether or not I should trust him. Like it or not I was stuck with him now, in this thing deep enough to know I wasn't going to get out until it was over. Now I had even more worries about how this was going to end. If Eddie hadn't already been dead, I'd have been tempted to kill him for putting me in this spot. Maybe I needed to be asking some questions of my own, just to clear at least a few details up between us. Right now things were clear as mud.

He edged past me before I could think of any good questions then stopped. I almost bumped into him again.

"That's a greenhouse."

"Yeah. I tore down the shed to put it up so I could start my landscaping business."

"You put the dead body of your ex-husband in a greenhouse."

I could see the beginnings of a smile on his face. It was the first thing that had made him look like a normal human since he got here.

"Well," I said, "at least he has flowers around him."

Matthias shook his head, and the smile vanished back into whatever part of his psyche he kept it in. I wondered if the flowers were as much benefit as I'd made it sound as we walked through them to the tarp in the center. Their sweet smell gave a very funereal aroma to the whole scene. The glow of the backyard light cast eerie shadows along the plastic walls. All we needed to complete things was some organ playing.

Not that any of it seemed to bother Matthias. He walked around the tarp, keeping his steady gaze on the floor and its display. If the sight of what he must know was a body bothered him, it didn't show. One of the perks of his business, I guess. Or the fact that the lump was exactly that to him, a body. Not a memory.

His focused gaze reminded me of what was about to happen. And of the questions I knew needed to be answered before it did. Matthias started to shift around me toward where Eddie lay, and I moved in front of him. He raised one dark eyebrow.

"About your fee."

"To raise him?"

"Yeah. We should settle everything up front,

before it happens."

"It?"

"Before things get, you know, started." *Why did I have to sound so flustered?* I may not be a power to be reckoned with, but I wasn't a novice. So why did I sound like a magickal moron?

"Okay." There was definite amusement in his voice. "Let's get everything settled."

"I just need to ask Eddie what happened. If you can get him, you know, coherent enough to answer, we can do it and get this over with in a jiffy."

"In a jiffy."

Why does everything I say sound so stupid when he repeats it like that?

"Well, I mean, I want this cleared up as soon as possible. Then I can take him back to the place where he was killed. You don't have to be involved in that."

"Are you going to leave him there?"

Well, duh. "Yeah. I mean, that's the whole goal of this, to get him out of my yard and away from me."

"Won't someone wonder why he's walking and talking but doesn't seem quite human?"

Oh, shit, I hadn't thought of that. "I guess maybe I'll need you then, too."

"I guess maybe you will." This time there was no mistaking the slight smile on his face. "I can get him walking and talking, as you say, at least for about twenty-four hours. The longer he stays above ground, the less…coherent he's going to be."

"Will he be coherent enough to answer questions? Will he know what happened to him and be able to tell me?"

"He'll be able to speak. He won't be especially

articulate right away."

"Eddie wasn't what you'd call articulate to start with."

"Then he'll sound like himself. At least for a while. It'll take an hour or so to get his speech up to speed, but then it will get better for a while. It should be long enough to answer your questions. As to what he knows, if he knows it he can tell you. If he doesn't…" He shrugged.

"Okay. Since I really want to get this over as soon as possible, then twenty-four hours shouldn't be a problem. So, how much would all that cost? The raising him, then putting him back, uh, under?"

This time it wasn't a smile that bothered me. The scary eyes were looking at me again, taking in my face in a way that made me want to run. But I was trapped between him in the doorway, and Eddie behind me. Talk about a rock and a hard place.

"I think we might be able to work out a trade."

"A trade?" Somehow I managed to keep the squeak out of my voice. "What kind of a trade?"

He leaned against the old wood workbench and folded his arms across his chest. "There is some business I need taken care of."

"Business?"

"Business that someone with your expertise in magick could help me out with."

Was now a good time to tell him that expertise and I weren't often on speaking terms? Nah. Still…

"Okay, a trade would be good."

I took a deep breath. All it did was add fuel to the flip-flops in my stomach. I'd never been one to flirt with danger like this, another reason to curse Eddie for this whole business. I was definitely in the frying pan. *So now was I about to jump into the fire?*

"Then we have a deal?"

"I think so. But I want things to be clear up front. I mean, there are some things I don't do."

"Fair enough." He nodded. "I can promise you nothing I need is illegal. Does that help?"

"Some. But if what you need turns out to be, shall we say, out of my area of expertise, what then?"

"You mean if you can't deliver the help I need."

It sounded way more dangerous when he put it like that. "Yes, if I can't deliver the help you need, what then?"

He ran a slow look up and down. I wish I could say the look made my body tingle with anticipatory sexual delight, but what I actually did was shiver. The only heat that popped into my mind came from memories of Aunt Anya's lectures on the fires of Hell. He smiled, not a comforting sight at all.

"I think we can work something out that would be mutually satisfactory."

Preferably something that left my body in one piece.

With that predatory walk, he backed me up until I finally got smart and stepped out of the way. He moved past me to the tarp. Kneeling down, he reached out a hand then paused.

"I will warn you though, if it turns out you had anything to do with your ex-husband's murder, all bets are off."

Though he hadn't turned those scary eyes back to me, the threat was definitely there. I swallowed hard.

"Fair enough."

Chapter Five

I was still on my feet, and I hadn't puked. Things were going well so far. At least so long as I didn't watch what was going on in front of me too closely. So long as I didn't think about what had happened in the last two hours. Also, if I didn't think about what might happen if this whole thing derailed. Yeah, maybe things weren't going so well after all.

Matthias circled Eddie's body, his movements measured and sure. The candles I'd set at the four directions threw his shadow into weird shapes on the wall. Herbs, he'd asked for, were scattered around the tarp. I winced at the crunching sound his boots made as he walked. I deep-breathed through my mouth and tried to tell myself it was just like being an extra in a B movie. Only the power I felt starting to surge through the room was all too real. *What in the hell was I about to see?* I ignored the small voice in my head screaming at me to run away and fast, but it wasn't easy, mainly because the small voice made a lot more sense than anything else. There were facets of the Craft I avoided for reasons I felt were good ones. Something told me my avoiding days were numbered.

Matthias paused over the bloody mess that was the man I had once loved. After a moment, he glanced up at me.

"Wash his face."

"Excuse me?" The words made me realize I'd hoped he'd forgotten I was there. *Or at least didn't want my help.*

"Easier to do it now than later. He might not be too cooperative after."

"After?" I shook my head, knowing I had to get the fog out of my brain.

"And if he looks in the mirror, all that might freak him out." He motioned to the blood on Eddie's face. "Sometimes they get scared and disoriented. Makes them harder to deal with."

"If I wash his face, I might freak out." It's damn lucky I haven't already, I thought. But I kept that part to myself. "Besides, Eddie's always hard to deal with."

He gave me that patient stare again. I wondered how long it would last, how long before he got up and walked out of here, washing his hands of the whole job. Get a grip, Rose.

I swallowed hard. "Sorry, I'm not being very helpful, am I?"

"No."

"Look, I'm not really used to this. You were probably expecting that I was, and maybe I should be. It's just that, well, there are things that don't, um, intrude, I guess you'd say, on my life. I mean, I'm committed to the Craft, don't get me wrong. And Alexis is a wonderful mentor and there's so much she's taught me, but we really haven't covered things of this, um, nature."

The babbling fairy had hit me again. My brain resisted the voice screaming shut up inside my head. "This is all probably something I should know. Or something I should be comfortable with anyway. But

I'm not. I mean I don't. I mean…" I waved a hand around me helplessly and sighed. "Maybe I am just a magickal moron."

"A magickal moron?" This time it wasn't patience on his face. For some strange reason he looked like I had said something that intrigued him.

"An idiot where these kinds of things are concerned." I hugged my arms around my waist and started to pace. "Sorry if that's a disappointment, if I'm a disappointment, but that's the way it is. I guess I was kind of hoping you'd come out here and do your thing, while I waited inside."

"Do my thing?"

"Yeah. I mean, you'd raise Eddie, I'll ask him some questions, he tells me where and then you do your thing again and…"

"Bada bing, it's over."

"Exactly."

"You're a student of Alexis Delacourte?"

Dammit, we'd already covered that. "Yes, a student. That being the operative word."

"For how long?"

Damn, I should have told him I was 25. "Three years."

He looked at me and back down at Eddie.

"Look, I don't get out much." I gave him a lame smile.

He stared back at me with the odd look on his face again.

I started over. This time from the beginning. Maybe that would do the trick. "What I mean is, this is a really small town. I'm your basic small-town hedge witch. I do herbal stuff, astrological charts, love spells for fuck's sake. Not this. Nothing like this."

I smudged one hand down the front of my jeans, leaving a smear of blood on my thigh. My eyes filled with threatening tears as I lifted my hands and stared at them. I took a deep cleansing breath before I spoke again.

"There's not much call here in my little world for anything big or spectacular. So I guess you can say this has sort of freaked me out. Much as I'd like to give a better impression, the truth is I'm scared shitless, my head is spinning like a crazed top, and I'm really thankful I haven't thrown up in front of you yet."

Matthias rose, moving to stand between me and what was left of Eddie. He shifted so my gaze had to focus on him.

"Not many ex-husbands to be raised, huh?"

There was the tiniest hint of sympathy in his voice. Or maybe I just imagined it. There was none on his face.

I shook my head. "No, most people like them to stay where they're put. When one of them has a little help getting to the dead state, it's usually the spouse who helped them. They don't want them back up and walking and talking."

"So being a practicing witch here in Mayberry doesn't afford you much training, is that the gist of what you're telling me?"

"That's pretty much it."

He looked as if he didn't believe me. Why, I had no idea. I'd told him the truth, that I was your basic hedge witch, an herbalist with attitude. Nothing I'd ever claimed took me beyond that. It was all I'd ever wanted to be. *So why was I mentoring with Alexis?*

"Let me tell you a little about it, then." Matthias knelt down by Eddie again and motioned me over. "I need for you to stay here with me. To raise a zombie, there has to be a bond between them and the living."

"And you're that bond?"

"I can be. To keep Eddie within the circle I raise him in would be no problem. But to break the circle, to take him outside of it as you propose, poses a different set of issues. And the need for a very secure bond."

"So how do you make it tighter?"

"It helps to have someone he had a bond with while he was living, someone to tie him to along with me. Someone who can call on that old earthly bond to help control him."

"You mean me?"

"Marriage is a powerful bond. Eddie did say 'I do' to you at the altar, right?"

He had. I'd rewound the wedding video and played it for him every time I confronted him about his cheating. I think we could both recite the entire thing by heart.

"But Eddie and I have been divorced for some time."

"Marriage is still a vow. A vow that generally gets, um, consummated, which creates an even greater bond."

We'd definitely done that, before marriage, during marriage and one night in a dreadful drunken stupor, right after the divorce. A sudden terrible thought struck me.

"Sex isn't a bond all by itself, is it?"

"It can be."

All sorts of terrifying images of Eddie running

amok all through town, telling everybody he met everything he could filled my head. I couldn't keep tabs on the man when we were married. How the hell was I going to do it now if half of the women in San Juan County had a bond with him?

Matthias stood up. "But I think we can keep him bound to the two of us only. It means you'll have to participate in raising him. You up to that?"

I swallowed again and nodded. "It's got to be done. Besides, I'm the one who called you."

"Yes, you did. You do know a binding spell I hope?"

My skills were deteriorating in his eyes, I could tell. "I know one. You do what you have to do, and I'll do my part." I took a deep breath and knelt down by Eddie. "If you want me to wash his face, I will. Whatever you need, I'll do it."

"Good. We'll make it a small circle to bring him back. No sense stretching things out too far until we see what kind of shape he's in."

I nodded. "There's water in the sink there. I can take care of…washing him. Just let me get a rag first."

Matthias gripped my arm as I passed. "Just get it and put the rag and the water beside him. We're going to cast the circle, get that wall of protection up now. It'll make it easier."

Like something could make any of this easier? I got the water, resisting the urge to toss some of it on my face. Trying not to stare down at him, I placed the items beside Eddie. As I stood up, I glanced over at Matthias. He nodded to me, that strange look back on his face. I knew there were some people who went into a trance state to do magick. I wondered if Matthias was one of them.

Swallowing the butterflies in my stomach, I started to walk the circle, pulling the energy up from the earth below just like Granny Claire taught me. Her words formed in my head and my lips moved with them. Thinking of her kept me grounded. She'd taught me to cast my circle as a child, taught me the importance of being careful and respectful of the magick. My parents had frowned on her teaching me about the Craft, but she managed to pass on some things. As I got older, I was able to ask more questions when my folks weren't around. Until she died.

I wondered what the magick thought of me now. Then I felt it slip around me, felt it complete what I'd called into existence. For a moment my world teetered in front of my eyes, safe, familiar and I started to relax into the flow of it. Before I could get comfortable, the power slammed a fist into my gut, and everything changed, reformed into something not at all comforting.

I stood inside what should've been a familiar wall of protection, a spot where I could fall back into being a simple hedge witch, doing a simple spell. But everything felt more energized, stronger, more powerful than any circle I'd ever cast. Energy snapped around me, calling to something inside me, something I'd never known was there before. A presence touched me that felt dimly familiar, though I couldn't put a name to it. It wanted me to name it, that much I could tell. To name it and to own it. As if it were already mine, simply waiting to be recovered from some sort of Wiccan baggage claim. It didn't make sense that this power, this presence, could have anything to do with me. My magick was safe. The screaming voice inside my head told me this magick was anything but safe. This magick was all about power. Tremendous power.

"Here."

I jumped at the sound of Matthias' voice, forced back into my own body for a moment. The strange magick bubbled around me, held back by a force I somehow knew came from Matthias. He stood holding a dampened rag. I reached for it like a life raft. Touching the wet cloth helped calm the raging forces inside me, water taming water, I suppose.

Steadying my nerves, I leaned down and wiped the rag over Eddie's face, trying not to gag. I closed my eyes and thought about the beach, my favorite place, and not about the feel of my ex-husband's lifeless body beneath my hand. After I'd managed a couple of swipes, I stood.

As I turned to Matthias, the energy surged again. With slow steps he began retracing my circle. It took a moment before I realized what he was laying down to add to the energy bounding the edges of it. It was blood. His own blood. I had never done blood magick before. Granny had, and she tried once to show me a little, to teach me about that kind of energy. But my mother had walked in on the lesson and freaked. After Granny died I didn't want any part of learning anymore about it. Now and then Alexis brought the subject up, but I ignored her. The tension in the pit of my stomach as I watched Matthias' blood drip onto the concrete made me remember why. Then I looked up at his face and my stomach did a full-on roll. I wanted to rub my eyes and make sure of what I was seeing, but another part of me thought moving might attract too much attention from the magick building in the tiny space.

The tattoo covering Matthias' face was moving, writhing beneath his skin like a trapped animal waiting to burst out. For a brief moment, I swore I saw a three-D image of a serpent rising like smoke around him, curling closer and closer to where Eddie's body lay as it unwound. Before I could be sure of what I saw, the image was gone, and the tattoo was nothing more than colors on his skin again. Everything inside me started shaking, but I knew it was too late to stop the things I had started.

Blood splattered on the floor from the crosswise cut Matthias had made in his left arm. And more dripped from the wicked-looking knife he carried in his right hand, the blade letting drop after drop leak down to bind the circle tighter with life and energy. Drop by drop, step by step, he took what I had created and fed it, raising the circle to a level I'd never seen before. Never found myself surrounded by before. It sparked around me, sucked at my feet as if the ground were giving way beneath me. My stomach rolled with it, and I swallowed hard.

Then Matthias spoke. He leaned over Eddie's face, saying the words again. That deep voice pulled at me, and I could tell Eddie had the same response. The man's power obviously lay in his ability to move people with the sound of his voice. Eddie's eyes flickered, and I swallowed hard. *You can do this, Rosalie Maria DeSalvo.*

Matthias moved a hand in front of him. Eddie's unfocused gaze followed it as he laid his still bleeding arm onto Eddie's mouth. His eyes closed, Eddie sucked at the blood. This time I wasn't sure I wasn't going to throw up. The noises went on for what seemed like hours before Matthias moved his arm away and stood.

"Edward DeSalvo, do you hear me calling to you?" Again the deep voice moved something inside me.

Eddie's eyes flickered open, and his bruised lips moved but no sound came out, a problem that cleared right up when his wandering gaze landed on me.

"Shit!"

Chapter Six

Okay, so it wasn't exactly the first word I expected from my first zombie. But at least it was familiar. It was the same word I heard from Eddie every time I caught him doing something he shouldn't be. Sort of his all-flavor cuss word.

I cleared my throat and tried for a smile. "Hi, Eddie."

"Ro…Rose?" His voice had a gravelly edge that hadn't been there before, and there was a nauseating wheeze that accompanied the words.

"Yeah, it's me. Um, just take it easy." I started to pat his shoulder then pulled back, not certain I should touch him yet. Or at all.

Eddie gazed around, his unfocused eyes flitting from spot to spot, I assume, looking for something familiar. Something besides me. Guess I didn't feel quite safe to him. Little did he know. But we could wait to spring that on him for a minute. I managed to keep quiet for a while as Matthias walked Eddie through his return to the world of the living. It took some time, but Eddie gradually began forming the strange sounds coming from his torn throat into words. Slow words, but words. Maybe this was going to work after all. Eddie looked around him. I saw a flicker of memory in his eyes.

"What the…? Where…? Why…?" Confusion

clouded his gaze as he seemed to be trying to grasp at the memory. Eddie tried to turn his head then stopped as his torn skin protested the movement. "What's…going on?"

"I was hoping you could tell me that, Eddie."

"Wha…" His wandering gaze finally focused on Matthias. "Who's he?"

"Your bridge." Matthias' voice was calm but commanding. Eddie squirmed under his gaze, like he wanted to say something but didn't. Or couldn't. Maybe this bond thing would work after all.

Eddie spoiled my high hopes with what I guess passed for a chuckle. The sound made me want to hurl. It looked like it had the same effect on him. "Want…orgy, Rose? Hope I'm up for it."

If it hadn't been for the thought of touching all that blood, I might have smacked the stupid grin off his face. Instead, I responded with temper, just like I always did with Eddie.

"You're not *up for* anything, Eddie. As a matter of fact, until a little while ago, you were *down under* my rosebushes."

Behind me, Matthias cleared his throat. I took a deep breath and tried to remember I was a witch, not a bitch. At least not always.

"Huh?" Eddie started to get to his feet. "Ow!"

I hauled one of my fancy new lawn chairs over to him. "Eddie, why don't you just sit still? I mean, just sit here."

Matthias gave a slight shake of his head and moved to help Eddie to a sitting position. I could read the what-the-hell-did-I-get-myself-into look even on his poker face. Or maybe my psychic power just decided to kick in. He bent down and spoke low and clear in Eddie's face.

"We need to talk, Eddie."

Eddie tried to focus on Matthias but clarity had never been his strong point. He blinked at Matthias. "Who…you?"

"Matthias. I'm a friend, Eddie. And we need to talk, the three of us."

Something bumped my hand, and I jumped. Matthias handed me a mirror.

"Make some noise, will you!" I snapped.

He sighed and motioned to Eddie with a nod.

"Eddie—" I stuck the mirror out in front of him. "—you need to look at something."

"Mirror? C'mon, Rose. 'S me."

"Just look, Eddie."

I held the mirror in front of him and watched his face. Shock didn't even begin to cover it. He stared at the image as if it were a bad horror flick, and he couldn't turn away. Then he looked up at me.

"Eddie…" I made my voice as gentle as I could. "I need you to tell me what happened, Eddie. To tell me who…" I closed my eyes, wishing there was a kinder way to say this. "Who killed you, Eddie?"

I could tell when it finally hit him, when he accepted my words as reality. His mouth fell open, and his shoulders slumped. I felt a twinge of sympathy and wished I could comfort him. What could it be like to have to be told you were dead?

"Eddie, I know this is hard."

He shifted away from me, and my suspicious nature went on alert.

"You've got to tell us what happened."

I watched his face and spotted all the signs right away. He fidgeted, refused to look me in the eye, all the old familiar reactions he had when he didn't want to tell me something. When the words out of his mouth were going to be a lie.

"Eddie, we need to know. You've got to tell us."

Matthias leaned against the old worktable. "Eddie," his calm voice had Eddie turning to him. "Who killed you?"

Eddie stared at the ceiling, and my stomach started doing flip-flops. He shrugged.

"Don't know."

Eddie looked down at the ground and mumbled the words. I nearly dropped the mirror in his lap as I stared at him.

"What?"

"Don't know." He shrugged as if he'd just told me he didn't know how he'd forgotten our anniversary or how he missed yet another day of work.

"What do you mean you don't know who killed you? Eddie, that's not possible. There's no way even you could've missed somebody hacking your face up."

Eddie flushed and looked away. "It was dark."

I got right up in his face so he could see the steam coming out of my ears. Matthias took a step back. Guess he was both brains and brawn.

"Don't mess with me, Edward DeSalvo."

I gave Eddie the look, the one I'd honed to perfection during our marriage. He winced.

"You did not turn up buried on my front lawn all by your lonesome. And there's no way you're gonna make me believe you don't know what happened. We're not talking about Jenna Riley's lipstick on your collar or Sylvia Woodard's earring in your backseat. This is your life and you damn well know who took it. And you're damn well gonna tell me."

"Maybe…there was some…trouble."

"You think? Who was it, Eddie? Who'd you screw this time?"

"Was gonna do it. Just…how could something that…ugly be married to…pretty woman like Belinda?"

The steam coming out of my ears must have hit him. Eddie even managed to look slightly guilty when he stared at me.

"I'm dead, huh?"

Even though I knew deep down he was playing on my sympathy, the temper building inside me blew out on a breath. "Yeah, Eddie. I'm so sorry."

"Thought…felt…worse than usual."

"Who did this to you, Eddie? Who were you working for?" Matthias' calm voice was a welcome sound.

Eddie swallowed hard, gagging a bit on the lacerated blood and bone around his throat. He put his head down before he spoke, and I found myself grateful for that. Between the grisly mess of his face and the sheer weirdness of listening to those old familiar excuses come out of a very dead face, I wanted to do some gagging of my own.

"Tony Espinosa."

This time I didn't gag, I almost spewed.

Chapter Seven

"Eddie, why? Why would you do something that stupid?"

It was at least the tenth time I'd asked it even though I knew all too well the answer. Eddie only did anything that involved money or sex or preferably both.

After my meltdown at Eddie's revelation of the likely person behind his demise, Matthias decided we needed to move the conversation into the house. He said Eddie needed a more familiar environment. I could have told him Eddie wasn't all that familiar with the kitchen, but it seemed like a moot point. I'd been bitchy enough already.

It wasn't an easy move. Eddie seemed to be having difficulty remembering the art of walking. His movements jerked so badly Matthias and I had to manhandle him along the walkway. And in the harsh fluorescent light of the kitchen, he looked even worse. I hollered for Leon, but apparently he was still sleeping it off. Mama was asleep on the couch. She mumbled something vaguely obscene when I let out my yell then turned over and started snoring again.

I dug a hooded jacket out of Leon's laundry for Eddie then spent ten minutes talking him into changing out of what was left of his favorite western shirt. I ended up helping him zip the hoodie over the shirt and called it good. That was all my stomach would handle.

At least most of the blood and slash marks were covered.

The three of us sat at the old kitchen table, Matthias and I with cups of Mama's black coffee. Eddie kept glancing over at our cups. I wondered if the smell bothered him or if it was the fact that he couldn't have any. I shook my head. I couldn't believe I was sitting in my kitchen at four in the morning trying to fix yet another Eddie mess. Matthias stared at Eddie with a look I couldn't identify. I didn't think I'd like what was going on behind that exotic face.

"Espinosa hired you for a job?"

Eddie nodded in answer to Matthias' question, and I wished he hadn't. Things moved that really shouldn't have.

"Said…do him favor. Help out…with…client."

"You promised that thug a favor?"

My voice hit a pitch I hadn't thought it could reach, and Matthias took the shaking coffee cup out of my hand. He set it down before wrapping his fingers around mine.

"Anthony Espinosa? The Anthony Espinosa? The one with ties to all the major Mexican cartels? The one who owns at least one judge in every county in New Mexico? And at least two police officers in every town and city from here to the Texas border? The one the feds have been trying to nail for the last two decades? The one…"

"I think that's who he's talking about," Matthias interrupted. "Judging by the unique shade of green he's turning. Something, I might add, I've never seen a zombie do."

I glared at Eddie. It was true. He looked a sick

shade of puke green, his torn face mottled with spots of it. It took a couple of deep breaths, but I managed to get my voice down to a lower octave.

I saw the anger in Eddie's eyes as he puffed his chest out, which was not a pretty sight in the condition it was in. "He asked…by name…for me. Needed… move product…needed somebody with…class. Wasn't no blow or nothing. Was…important, real valuable. Said client knew me…my rep…asked me to handle…deal."

"Reputation? What reputation?"

"Mine," he rasped, the words coming out a bit stronger. "For getting the job done. Said I was…trustworthy." He moved a hand like he wanted to thump his chest then thought better of it.

"Eddie, you're not trustworthy. You're a lot of things, but not trustworthy. No way."

He started to pout again. I remembered I needed to get this cleared up so I could get back to my life. My life without Eddie in it. Perhaps I should take a different tact.

"Okay, Eddie, so this client of Espinosa's wanted you to do him a favor, and you didn't deliver, and he killed you for it."

He shook his head and fewer things flew off. Was he drying up, I wondered? "You…didn't deliver."

"What!"

Eddie leaned back in the chair. Getting dead had made him more cautious. "Well, promised him…"

"Promised him what?"

"Sale…you were going to sell him something."

"You promised some stranger I'd sell something for him?"

He shook his head again, and I wasn't sure it was going to stay on this time. "To him. You sell to him. Or, give it back to him."

"Sell or give, Eddie, which is it?" Matthias interrupted before I had the chance to. Guess he saw the look on my face.

"Said…family heirloom. Said…your granny kept it. He wants it back…for his family. Wants to pay for it. Big time money."

"Money you, of course, took up front." I knew Eddie well enough to know the answer to that one.

Eddie nodded. "Some of it. I was going to bring it to you, to show you his…good will."

"So you were supposed to wave some money in my face, and I'd say sure thing to whatever he wanted to buy?"

Eddie nodded, looking almost pleased. His words and the squishy sound the nod made left me anything but pleased. I jerked my hand from Matthias' grip and covered my eyes.

Matthias didn't try to take my hand again. "Eddie, who was this client?

"Don't know." Eddie shrugged. "Tony just passed on what he wanted to me."

"Because this client asked for you."

"Yeah. By name."

I heard the note of pride in the gravelly voice and wanted to smack him. "Why, Eddie, is this the first I've heard of any of this and what in the all-living hell could some rich guy want to buy from me? Granny didn't have anything that valuable, at least not to a stranger. Not valuable enough to hire Tony Espinosa to go after it."

All the talking must have kickstarted Eddie's faculties because he seemed to sit a bit straighter and his words came out a bit clearer. I knew it shouldn't but it started me hoping he'd know what I needed to hear and I could still clear this whole thing up without me ending up serving a long prison sentence.

"I was working up to it. You're not easy, Rose, talk to. Don't give time to explain."

"This working up to telling me, was that the reason behind the sudden appearance of two new rosebushes and the Christmas card you sent this year, something you never did the entire time we were married?"

"Yeah." He didn't seem to see anything wrong in that. Dead, but the same old Eddie.

"So, you never said anything to me."

There was no mistaking the guilty look on his face. "I sort of got delayed."

"You sort of got laid you mean. Seems to me I remember hearing you took up with Jenna Riley again not long after Christmas."

"Jenna inherited…bunch of money from her grandma. Said…always wanted to see Caribbean. I said okay. By the time we got back, Tony's all pissed off. Said twenty-four hours to get the cup thing for him or else. Scared me, but then Belinda came over—"

"Belinda? What happened to Jenna?"

I don't know why I even bothered to ask. Maybe because it was an old habit I hadn't broken yet.

"Never mind, don't answer that."

Since he didn't look like he planned on answering, Eddie ignored me.

"Things got going good till Tony called. Sent guys over to…help me. Belinda's big ass boyfriend one of

'em and—" Eddie looked down at the mirror. "Well…"
He gave a sort of shrug.

"A cup?" I stared at him. "This is all about a cup?"

"Crazy, huh? Guy says he gave it to your granny
when they were courting."

"Courting?" Now it was my turn to be confused.

"She never gave it back. Guess 'cause she was sort
of like you."

"Sort of like me?"

"All the witchy stuff. It's magickal cup, he says.
Needs it back." Eddie snorted. "Got more money than
he deserves." Guess his opinion of my Craft hadn't
changed.

"If he gave it to her then she should've kept it. It
was hers. Courting? Who is this guy? A magickal cup?
What is this guy?"

"I was just…middle man. Witchy woohoo
stuff…your thing."

"Trust me, Eddie. You've done more witchy
woohoo stuff tonight than I ever have."

I couldn't resist the jab at him. Well, I could have,
but I didn't want to. Behind me Matthias cleared his
throat. Truthfully, I'd almost forgotten anyone else was
there. The conversation with Eddie had been way too
familiar.

I got up and paced to the door. After all the pacing
I'd done tonight, I shouldn't have to worry about that
five pounds Mama hinted at earlier. Matthias came up
behind me and put his hand on my arm. Something
inside me jumped, or maybe sizzled. Magick still clung
to him.

"It seems we're not going to get any useful answers
until we find out who this client was."

"You mean the person who killed him? That's who you want to look up?" I stared at him like he was crazy. "I don't think we need to be doing that. Let the crazy guy get somebody else's cup. There are antiques stores in town that have got way better stuff than anything Granny Claire had." I started pacing again. "No, we need to put Eddie back somewhere."

Eddie gave me a funny look. "Huh?"

Matthias shook his head. "Did you really understand what you were asking for when you called me? How did you think you were going to return Eddie to the scene of the crime without finding out who killed him and why? Wasn't that the purpose of all this, to find who killed him? Somewhere in the equation you had to know you'd run across a murderer. Someone who might not want you returning Eddie. The same someone who planted his body in your front yard."

"Know? I don't know anything. You say that like this whole thing was thought out beforehand. FYI, there wasn't a whole lot of planning in this. In case you can't tell, I'm winging it. Going on impulse. I just wanted Eddie to tell me whose front yard to put him in. I figured his killer was some pissed off husband or boyfriend. Or even some woman. At the very least I hoped for somebody who was as drunk as him when it happened."

"Wasn't drunk."

"Be quiet, Eddie." I glared at him.

"You counted on it being somebody who wouldn't say or remember anything."

I turned my glare to Matthias. "Yeah, that's the way it should have worked. Nothing I've thought of so far included a face to face with his killer."

Matthias' face got one of those scary looks as he grabbed my arm and shook me just a bit. "Then you better start thinking harder."

With a deep breath, he released my arm. I resisted the urge to rub it. He glanced over at Eddie, who was back to staring in the little hand mirror.

"Look," he began. "Maybe a talk with Tony would be a good first step."

"Are you crazy? A first step to the last day of our lives. You don't call Tony Espinosa up and tell him you want to chat, not even if the topic is a good one. And, call me crazy, did he kill one of his men probably falls in the not-a-good-topic category."

He looked like he wanted to shake me again, harder this time. "It's either go to him or have him come to you. I'm betting his client still wants whatever this cup is, and both of them are still going to be looking your way to get it."

"Oh, thanks for the comfort. I thought you were here to help me solve this problem, not enlarge it."

Mr. Patient just kept staring at me. I took a deep breath and tried to calm down.

"Sorry. That wasn't fair. I dragged you into this, and now I'm demanding you fix it all."

"I've always found it better to take the offensive. Defensive positions never work out well with people like that."

I took another look at Eddie. I'd been on the defensive since Leon stumbled over him tonight, and Matthias was right, things so weren't working out well. I still needed to find a new burial ground for Eddie, and short of sneaking into Mr. Murray's garden and planting him under the potatoes, I needed to find out where to put him. I was giving the potatoes serious consideration when Matthias spoke again, low enough for Eddie not to hear.

"There is one thing I may not have made clear."

Oh great. I looked from Eddie to him. "And that would be?"

"Eddie can't just be buried anywhere. Once you've taken him from death, you're obligated to either put things to right before you hand him back or put him back where you found him. So he either goes back to where he died or he goes back in your front yard."

"What!"

He shrugged. I wondered if the gesture was the male answer to anything they didn't want to admit they'd done.

"That's the way it works. I thought you knew the boundaries. You're Alexis' student."

Yeah, and she and I are going to have a really long chat very soon. "No, I didn't know that."

I plopped down on a chair and tried to ignore Eddie's wheezing. Prison sounded a lot safer than a visit with Tony Espinosa. With a jury I could probably play up the poor pitiful me factor, maybe even throw in a few tears and get it down to manslaughter. Rumor was Tony had offed his last wife 'cause she burned dinner. Before I could pick it up to turn myself in, the phone rang.

Chapter Eight

Still debating life behind bars, I snarled a hello before I thought to wonder who would be calling me so early in the morning.

"Should I take it from your greeting that you have discovered my little message, Mrs. DeSalvo?"

The voice was cultured and deep. Definitely not Tony Espinosa. Besides, I didn't think Tony ever used the phone for business. Up close and personal was more his style from what I'd heard. Matthias must have noticed the look on my face because he reached over and hit the button for speaker phone. It took a few seconds to get my throat to work and when it did, what came out was more of a croak than a word.

"Message?"

"Perhaps I was wrong, then. I assumed it would be quite clear. Unless my delivery did not go as ordered. Have you seen your husband recently, Mrs. DeSalvo?"

"Who is this?"

"Ah, you have seen him."

A bad feeling crept along my skin. Murderers shouldn't sound so elegant. A tiny spark of anger rode the wave of a long and crazy night into my brain. It set fire to my sense of safety, which was already on wobbly legs. The words slipped out before I could stop them.

"You know what they say about assuming."

"Indeed?"

I heard the tiniest bit of surprise under the word. Guess I could either fold up and start whimpering or hope I could keep surprising him. I'm very good at bluffing, and the nausea had passed. Time to try something new.

"Never mind, it's probably beneath you. Back to my question. Who is this?"

The voice had gone back to elegant. "I would prefer we do our introductions face to face. It is a bit more civilized."

"Civilized? You've got to be kidding me."

"Indeed, no. My preference would have been to conduct all our business in a civilized manner."

"I don't think that word means what you think it means. FYI, people who want to be civilized don't do business with guys like Tony Espinosa."

"Although I'm sure your attempts at humor should be appreciated, I believe I would prefer to get to the serious side of our conversation. The night is almost over, and neither of us have gotten what we want yet. As to my methods, Mr. Espinosa was merely a reference guide."

"A reference guide?"

"An unfortunate step in the process of recovering my property. Alas, I was disrupted in my attempts to meet you, hence the need for my rather unpleasant delivery."

Mr. Master of Understatement. And yet another man who remained cool, calm and collected at all times. I was getting pretty tired of people like that. Besides, my brain was definitely not up to riddles. I looked over at Matthias, but his expression was unreadable, at least by an amateur like me. I cleared my throat, refusing to look over at Eddie. I knew what expression would be on his face. Death hadn't changed him much. I went back to winging it, hoping I could find the words to make myself look at least collected, if not cool and calm. I worked better angry anyway.

"As you've obviously discovered, I'm in the book. Maybe you should've tried that first. Beats having the bodies pile up every time you need to talk to someone."

The voice chuckled. "Edward did say you were a very, um, direct woman. And somewhat difficult to deal with."

"So you thought this would soften me up?"

"I wanted your full attention. And I prefer not to waste time. My business is quite urgent."

"Urgent?" *Not nearly as urgent as mine, buddy.*

"Believe me, such a crude method would not have been my first choice. Once we become acquainted, you will know I am usually a man of great finesse, and you will understand I am also quite tenacious and somewhat direct myself."

"I'm beginning to understand a lot. But I have to tell you, Mr.?"

"As I said, Mrs. DeSalvo, I believe it would be better for us to do our introductions in person."

"Not likely. Especially after your little message. As a matter of fact, your message tempts me to go to the police instead of dealing with you."

"And what would you tell them?"

I opened my mouth and closed it again. So much for bluffing.

"Ah, it is a difficult question, is it not? Going to the police would not be in your best interests. And, as enjoyable as it is for me to know that a man of my age can still tempt a pretty young woman, I must urge you to resist that particular reaction. For if you are anything like your grandmother, you are nowhere near glib enough to convince them you played no part in this."

My heart skipped a beat. "My grandmother? What do you know about my grandmother?"

"Claire was an interesting woman. She was not, however, a woman with great persuasive skills. Claire preferred the direct route when it came to her speech. It was a trait that often made things difficult."

"An innocent person doesn't have to be persuasive. They have the truth on their side."

"Ah, the truth."

"You're not a big believer in the truth?"

"Perhaps you are more naïve than your husband led me to believe, Mrs. DeSalvo."

"Ex-husband, so quit with the Mrs. DeSalvo shit. And I'm not naïve."

"Inexperienced, then. The truth is not always the appropriate weapon. There are many who have told it and found they were not believed by your trusted police."

"Why wouldn't they believe me? I would hardly murder my ex-husband, bury him in my own front yard, and then report it, now would I?"

"Sometimes the most obvious is also the easiest. I would not count on the local law enforcement to not jump at the opportunity to wrap up an ugly murder with the easiest solution. That could be dangerous."

"And you're not dangerous?"

"I want what is mine, and I have no real desire to murder for it. Believe it or not, your husband's death was accidental, not intentional."

"Ex-husband. So it was only planting him in my yard that was intentional."

"It served the double purpose of cleaning up a mess and bringing the two of us together. I am a businessman. I appreciate a bargain."

"So now you want me to walk right up to you and talk about business or else I'm stuck with hiding Eddie for the rest of my life. Is that it?"

"Meeting with me can serve your purpose as well."

"So could taking my chances with the police."

"Ah, but you should never leave your future to chance. One never knows what chance might bring. My home is not far from you. It shouldn't take you more than an hour or so to get here."

He gave me detailed instructions as I rummaged in the kitchen drawer for a pencil.

"I'll be expecting you. Oh, and feel free to bring your friends, if it makes you feel any safer."

The phone clicked, and I fumbled behind me for a chair. Matthias pushed the closest one up to my knees. I flashed him a grateful smile as I sank down into it.

"Sounds like our argument is solved."

Matthias' matter-of-fact demeanor was starting to get on my nerves. And they were already pretty jangled. He sat down beside me and gave me one of his looks.

"Yes it is," I mumbled. "We throw some things in a suitcase, and we all get the hell out of here." I looked at him and realized he hadn't run for the door. "He doesn't know you're here. I'll promise to pay up if I live through this. You should go home."

Matthias stared at me with the scary eyes. It made me want to squirm. Better that I insult him than get him killed, I thought. Eddie shuffled by me toward the living room.

"Eddie, where are you going?" I couldn't keep the irritation out of my voice.

He jerked his head toward the living room. "TV."

As if that explained it all, he walked through the door. I shook my head. The whole weird night hit me, and I couldn't stop the laugh. Hysteria bubbled out of me as I thought about my zombie ex-husband fumbling with the remote while the hottest guy I'd ever been close to looked like he wanted to find a strait-jacket. There was a shriek from the living room followed by a thwacking sound. I heard Eddie yelp a few seconds before Mama stormed through the door. She glared at me from the doorway. I laughed harder.

"That shit is not funny, Rosalie DeSalvo. This ain't Halloween, and you ought to give a body some warning before you let that…body come in there and scare me out of a sound sleep."

The look on her face slipped the last of my sanity, and I lost it. I laughed so hard I fell out of the chair. It was all I could do not to roll around on the floor. Matthias stood and moved back from me. Mama gave a snort and exited down the hall. I finally got a grip on myself and struggled to a sitting position. Matthias watched me from the sink.

"Feeling better?"

He still looked cool, calm and collected. Apparently dealing with a crazy woman, a zombie and a pissed off medium didn't make him break a sweat. I stared at him, all neat in his leather jacket and looking hotter than anyone had a right to. "It would be a damn shame to get you killed." The thought drove the last of the laughter from me. "You need to leave now.

He raised an eyebrow. "Are you firing me?"

"I'm saving you. Whoever this is doesn't know you're here." I said it with the fervent hope it wasn't a lie. "Leave and he won't know."

"I beg to differ. And I was invited to this party. He did say you could bring your friends."

"We aren't friends. I dragged you out in the middle of the night to get Eddie up and talking, and you did it. You're done. If I don't live through this, I'll leave your payment in my will. Get out now and save yourself."

He reached over and poured another cup of coffee, like he hadn't a care in the world. Careful of the hot mug, he walked past me and set the cup on the table before turning around and grabbing my hands. His quick movement startled me, but before I could protest he had me off the floor and shoved into the chair in front of the mug. The restrained violence that vibrated through his touch kept my mouth shut. I looked from him to the coffee.

"Sit down, Rosalie."

I looked back up at him. "I think I already am."

"Good. Now you can shut up and listen to me."

"Okay." I blew on the coffee, thinking its heat might be the safer alternative.

"Do you honestly believe I take calls in the middle of the night from frantic women who want their dead ex-husbands raised?

When he put it like that, I started to wonder about things I probably should've thought of before I placed the call.

"I'm going to say no."

"Damn right. I'm not a doctor. I don't take calls

from strangers. My number's not in the phone book, and there is no ad listing what I do. Now tell me why I might not only take your call but come out here in the middle of the night?"

"I...don't know."

"Exactly." He walked to the counter where I'd left the directions my trembling hand had written. "There's a hell of a lot you don't know, Rosalie DeSalvo. A hell of a lot you should know that you don't know."

As he pulled me out of my chair, he slapped the paper in my hand.

"Tonight you start your education, witch. And the first test is here."

Chapter Nine

Covered in a cloak of shadowy moonlight, the red sandstone walls rose up like an extension of the desert sands, massive and elegant in an eerie sort of way. From the outside it looked to my overactive imagination like a tomb or an ancient Egyptian pyramid. Wonder what it looked like on the inside. I wasn't sure I was ready to find out. My nerves were already stretched pretty tight. Maybe this guy made a habit of burying people who pissed him off under flowerbeds. I had visions of dead bodies buried all around the house, fertilizing the beautiful southwestern landscaping I could see from the spotlights that dotted the roof. A thick wall surrounded the entire structure and the wide open, iron gate almost dared us to drive through.

We'd come in the fancy sports car. A shame to waste what should have given me a thrill in a good way on a night like this. But Matthias ruled out my driving. Guess my hands shaking on the phone convinced him it wouldn't be a good idea to put a steering wheel in them. I'd suggested we leave Eddie with Mama, an arrangement that didn't thrill either one of them. But Eddie had no intention of being left behind "like a kid". Guess not even death changed machismo. Since he kept coming out to the car every time we tried to leave, I just buckled him in the back seat and gave him my witch stare. It had no more effect on him now than it ever had. Keeping an eye on him while dealing with the person responsible for his passing didn't seem wise, but nothing I'd done this whole night gave off an air of intelligence so I guessed I'd roll with it. It was just another layer of WTF for a night that had been filled with it so far. Eddie might pretend he didn't know what had happened to him, but faced with the one who caused it, there was no telling what he'd do. Eddie was completely predictable about being unpredictable.

We edged to the gate, and Matthias let the car idle for a minute.

"Do you feel it?"

I didn't have to ask him what he meant. Even through my nerves, I felt the magick all around the place. Waves of energy pulled at me, with a wild force scary as hell. My reaction to it said something, considering all I'd already been through. It made me reconsider my definition of magick. This wasn't the benevolent flow I was used to. This was raw power, with true magick at its core. It resonated off the walls, off the land itself.

"He's got wards all over the place." I shivered. "It's like an energy field around his whole house."

If it was meant to send a message, it did: *Enter at your own risk!* I leaned out of the window and gazed at the upper tower. *Rapunzel, Rapunzel, let down your hair.* Fairy tales seemed to be the only thing coming to mind. Grimm's fairy tales.

Matthias drove through the curved metal gate, and the moment he did, the energy sort of zapped around us. My skin vibrated with the urge to move, to find the source of that power and cloak myself in it. Good sense told me I'd better find a way to shake off its pull before I walked through the door. I glanced back at Eddie. He was occupied with keeping the seat belt from pulling off a few body parts. The night just couldn't seem to get better. Then I felt the eyes on me.

"He's watching us."

"Let him watch," Matthias answered. "It's good to know the balance of power before we walk in there."

I started to tell him there was an imbalance of power and none of it was on our side, but maybe I was wrong. Maybe. So I nodded instead. From behind the gate, a shadowy figure stepped out, and I screamed.

"Just a security guard, Rose."

Matthais rolled down the window. Behind me, Eddie made a strangled noise deep in his throat. *Dear Goddess, don't let this be the one who killed him. Let us please make it through the front door at least before it all explodes.*

The man moved toward the car, one hand resting on the gun at his hip. With a smile I knew couldn't be trusted, Matthias gunned the car and drove on to the house, leaving the man standing behind him. I watched to see if he raised his gun, but he only stared at us for a moment then walked back to the wall.

"That was kind of risky." I looked over at Matthias. He still wore the smile.

"Power plays usually are."

"Look—" I flicked a glance to the house then back to him. "—have I told you how sorry I am about this whole mess?"

"Repeatedly."

"I should never have dragged you into this."

"It'll teach me not to answer my phone after dark."

I opened my mouth to apologize again, and he shook his head.

"Kidding, Rose. I'm kidding. What I'm not kidding about is the fact that you need to calm down and focus. I need you ready for anything in there." He pulled the car to a stop in the circular driveway. "I know this place."

"You do?"

He nodded. "I thought I recognized the address when you wrote it down. Now that I see it, I know it's the place. And I've heard a bit about the guy who lives here."

"A bit?"

"Yeah. Some of this might be for show, but that doesn't mean he's not serious."

"Serious about what?"

"About getting what he wants."

I didn't know yet if I was grateful that Matthias pulled no punches or if I'd rather have someone a little less blunt by my side. He reached for my hand as I started to open the door.

"Make no mistake about that, Rose. Once you walk into that house, you've got bigger problems than getting Eddie back in the ground. You need to be prepared for that."

Okay, now I'd decided that I wished Matthias was less blunt. But I nodded anyway, as if I knew how to prepare myself for any of the things that had happened in the last few hours. *Was there a manual on this somewhere and if so, how the hell do I get a hold of a copy?*

For some strange reason I would ponder on many times after, I heard my Granny Claire's voice on the wind around me. It wasn't words so much as the sound of her voice, the tone she'd always used with me, powerful, yet full of wonder and love. It wrapped around me like a thick warm blanket against the sudden chill.

"What is it?" Matthias stared at my face.

I shook my head. "Nothing." As I started to move away he leaned in front of me.

"Rose, my power knows certain elements."

"What?"

He gave me an exasperated look. "I talk to the dead on a regular basis. I know when they are about, when they communicate with someone who's standing right next to me. If we're going in there together, then we need to do it together. Don't hide from me."

"I'm not hiding, I mean, not anything that's…I'm sorry. There's not really anyone in my life that I talk to about this stuff. Yes, I ask Alexis questions, but she's not there every day and even with Mama, I don't…" I looked up at him. He rolled his eyes.

"I'm doing it again, aren't I?"

"If you mean the babbling then, yes. We need to be on the same page, Rose, about everything, all the time, or one of us is going to screw this up."

I nodded. "You're right. It's just I'm so used to doing this alone that I didn't think about…well, about sharing, I guess. I'm not used to it."

Behind me Eddie snorted. Before he could get anything else out, I glared back at him. Matthias' voice forestalled any arguing.

"Get used to it, Rose. Neither of us needs to be walking blind right now."

"Okay, okay, I got your point." I started to move

away and Matthias gripped my arm.

"So?"

"Oh." I flushed a deep red. *Was I ever going to stop looking stupid in front of this guy?* "It was just my granny."

"Talking to you?"

"Not so much talking as just being here with me. Does that make sense?"

He nodded. "Protection. Love is a great protective spell."

I felt a tingle inside my heart at his words. Granny Claire had indeed loved me, maybe the only one who had known the real me and still loved. I could face anything knowing that. Surprised to find a bit of my fear gone, I straightened my shoulders and nodded to Matthias.

"Let's go inside this place and see just what we're up against."

****

When the door opened, I realized I'd expected someone like Lurch to answer. The woman was nearly as tall, but the resemblance ended there. One look at her told me she was everything I hated in beautiful women.

"Well, well, well. I guess I lose the bet."

Her smooth tone grated on my tension tight nerves. "Excuse me?"

"I told Armando you wouldn't show."

I stared at her. She stood six feet in stiletto heels. I'm betting the heels added three or four inches. That may have been jealousy more than fact. It still put her head and shoulders above me. It wasn't just height, either. Red curls tumbled down ivory shoulders left open for viewing by the low-cut black dress. A dress that yelled I have money, and I know how to spend it. She had curves, and she knew how to flaunt them, too. She couldn't have screamed SEX louder if she'd had a neon sign on her forehead.

"Please, come in."

The words had all the warmth and welcome of please, drop dead. Her painted on smile strained a bit as she moved back to let us through the door. Guess losing the bet pissed her off. Or it might have been that she spotted Eddie. When she saw him, she gave me a disgusted look and turned away.

I didn't want to look at Matthias' face as she led us into the hallway. Why torture myself watching him watch her ass? Then I felt his hand slide into mine. I looked up to find him staring at me, that now familiar unreadable expression on his face.

"Breathe, Rose. Just breathe."

I relaxed until I felt Eddie starting to move past me. When I turned I saw an unmistakable look on his face, one I had seen so many times I knew what it meant even through the mess that remained of his looks. His gaze was glued to Yvette's ass, and one hand reached up to slick back his hair.

"Oh, no you don't."

Matthias gave me a raised brow. I jerked my head toward Eddie. He rolled his eyes as Eddie strutted closer to Yvette, who stopped and looked back. Then she looked at me.

"Seriously?"

I nodded. She shook her head, then stared at Eddie. I noticed she didn't shudder or anything like that and that made me wonder what her date life was normally like. Eddie plastered on his best smile, and Yvette continued to stare. Eddie's smile faltered a bit as he closed his mouth. After another moment he lost the smile and stepped back behind me. Yvette shook her head before turning back around.

As if watching my dead ex-husband flirt with a woman who wanted to kill me wasn't enough to set my nerves dancing, the inside of the house matched the outside. I hate dark spaces, closed-in rooms and the feel that comes from too much stuff in too small a space. Not that these rooms were small. But the massive furniture and walls of paintings hemmed me in all the same. Not being an art critic, I could only guess at the value that lined the walls. Still, as beautiful as the paintings were, the effect of them towering over me left me feeling like a very small mouse in an elegant maze. I tried not to gawk, especially when I noticed the smirk on Red's face. As I racked my brain for a witty comment, a burst of laughter made me jump.

"Oh, how delightful. How absolutely delightful."

I turned to stare at the man in the doorway, whose gaze was riveted on Eddie. For a person of considerable bulk, he moved much too quietly.

"A zombie. You have made my evening, Mrs. DeSalvo. I had not expected it of you."

His smile grew broader as he looked from Eddie to me. I wanted to point out that I hadn't done it, but calling attention to Matthias didn't seem like a good idea at the moment.

"Thought I'd return the favor and give you something unexpected."

He laughed again. I'm such good entertainment. His outfit likely rivaled one of the paintings in value, elegant and tailored in a way that screamed money. He wore his clothing well, but what lay inside it was a different story. A painter worth his salt would have given his skin a bit more color. It looked like thick paper that had once had a rich golden tone to it and then had been left in a dark corner, far away from the sun for a very long time. All the gold had faded and what was left looked soured. Something not helped by the thick white hair that flowed down to his shoulders. His aristocratic features must have once been handsome, with eyes so dark they were almost black, aquiline nose and high cheekbones. Now he looked like a man who lived too well, who'd indulged his own desires for too long. There was a cruelty to his eyes and an arrogance to his smirk that showed a man used to getting what he wanted. It wasn't a far stretch to imagine him a murderer. He gave me the creeps. He'd said he had courted Granny Claire, but he looked to be a million years older than her. Maybe it was just that she was perpetually stuck at the age she'd died in my memory. I glanced over at Eddie, who was still staring at Yvette.

"Nice to know you're pleased with your handiwork, Vigil."

Matthias' voice held a spark of power that chilled me. He'd told me he recognized the house, but for some reason I hadn't thought to ask the name of the man we were here to meet. Stupid of me. Now I felt a bit left out of the conversation. From the look on Vigil's face, he'd forgotten all about me. It felt like being in the middle of a magickal pissing contest. Even Eddie looked from one to the other, picking up on the tension that wrapped itself between them.

I had been so busy dissecting the monster in front of me, I hadn't chanced a look at Matthias' face. I took a long one now and shivered at what I saw. The expression on it was not only readable it was damn near flammable. Even with what I'd felt in the greenhouse, I realized how much he had held back from me. Raw power and violence filled him. A red flag I should have noticed long before now waved to me out of the corner of my brain. Just who was Mr. M. Romero, and why had he agreed to come to my house so easily? Part of me wanted to protest that it hadn't been easy, or that it was what someone like him did. But I knew there was far too little I knew about the man I had adopted so quickly as my knight.

I shoved the warning to the back of my brain and focused on the scene in front of me. It felt a bit like being caught between duelers. Vigil gave an abrupt laugh, and the anger he'd been radiating eased off. Something told me it was only under wraps again, not gone.

"Ah, so you know who I am."

Matthias nodded. "I've heard of you."

"It is good to know my reputation precedes me, Mr. Romero. As does yours. I am also glad to see you accepted my invitation here tonight. I have looked forward to meeting you for some time."

I was beginning to feel superfluous to this little meeting. Vigil continued to play the staring game with Matthias for a minute more before turning his creepy gaze back to me. I couldn't tell if he thought he'd won the contest or had just decided to get on with things.

"My apologies, my dear. It's a foolish man who ignores a beautiful woman in the room. From the look you're giving me, I fear you do not share my humor. Your face is quite expressive, Mrs. DeSalvo. May I call you Rosalie?"

My name spilled out of his mouth in a way that made me gag. I'd never gone much for the whole Mrs., Ms., Miss thing. Seemed like just another way to put women in a neat little box so you didn't have to really get to know them. Just file them accordingly, interesting, not interesting, no way in hell. I'd grown cynical in my old age.

"I'd prefer we didn't get first name friendly." It wasn't hard to keep the cold touch in my voice. Everything inside me had gone cold the minute I walked through the door. "So since you know mine, now it's time to let me in on your name. Unlike my friend here, I have no idea who the hell you are."

"Then forgive me yet again. I am Armando Vigil. Welcome to my home."

He gave a low bow. What a perfect gentleman. Yeah, right.

"I hope you haven't been waiting long." He nodded to Red, who'd stopped in the adjoining doorway like a security guard ready to bar the way to the nosy tourists. "Yvette was kind enough to welcome you in while I cleared up some business so we could enjoy our visit uninterrupted."

"Enjoy our visit?" I gave him an incredulous look.

"I've arranged for a nice meal. Yvette, would you please tell Roger we're ready for him to begin serving?"

"Don't bother, Yvette." I emphasized her name as I gave her my best fake smile. "You dragged us here with threats and intimidation and now you want to sit and visit?" I shook my head. "We are so not going to sit down around the dinner table and chat. Forgetting for a moment the fact that you're a monster and a killer, I'm pretty sure any food I tried to eat right now would come back up. I'd hate to puke all over your pretty carpet."

He laughed. "How colorful you are, Mrs. DeSalvo. Not only have you brought a wonderful surprise with you in the form of your husband—" He gave Eddie a humorous look at the word *form.* "—but what spice your conversation will add to my evening."

What I wanted to add to his evening was more physical than verbal. Something that would wipe the phony look off his face. If I didn't know what he'd done, I'd think he was one of those people with more money than they knew what to do with so they looked for causes to support. Just a kind benefactor wanting to make you feel at home.

"Well, that's what happens when you let the poor folk in. They tend to add a little color to an otherwise bleak world." I turned to the door, Matthias' hand still gripped in mine. "We're out of here."

Before I could tug Matthias with me, his voice made me pause. What I saw on Vigil's face when I turned froze me in my tracks. There was nothing congenial about him now. That mask was gone, and the real thing scared the shit out of me.

"I'm afraid I must insist, Mrs. DeSalvo."

His voice felt heavy in my head, pushing at my will like a battering ram. Matthias must have felt it too for he moved up closer to me, his hand tightening on mine. Guess the real show was about to start. Vigil watched us in a way that let me know he knew the havoc he was playing with our heads. Yvette appeared to enjoy the game of cat and mouse way too much for my comfort. *Was she part of the power or just window dressing?* I didn't know the answer or even how important the question was.

"We have much to talk about, dear Rosalie, and as I mentioned earlier, there is a sense of urgency to our quest."

I felt him all the way down to my toes, like dark syrup dripping over everything inside me. It should have scared the shit out of me even more, and I knew in some part of me it did. But in another part, one I wasn't so familiar with, I felt anger like nothing I'd ever known before.

As the rage rose in me, I had an image of my grandmother, only she didn't look like the woman I loved. She looked like, well, she looked like someone you should be scared of because this woman could kick your ass. Violence filled her eyes, shot out of her like a fire that spread faster than you could stop it, hot, moving and deadly. And it took the magick coming from Vigil and ate it. No messing around, no negotiation, it ate it all down before Vigil could blink. For a moment, I saw surprise on his elegant face, but he masked it quickly, giving me an imperceptible nod. Like I had won at least the first round of whatever weird battle he had us engaged in.

I looked back at my grandmother's image, but she looked as she always had, safe and normal. I tried to cling to the safety that had always come with her presence, but it was slippery. I still wanted to scream or to run for the most part. But I also wanted to put my hands on Vigil, to hurt him for what he had done. I curled my fingers around Matthias', making a fist of both our hands. To my surprise the feel of our joined hands reassured me, sort of like the whole strength in numbers thing. I found myself no longer afraid of hurling. I wanted to do some damage instead. Some latent sense of unfamiliar violence lived within me and wanted out—wanted out bad. Then I became aware of the soft whisper growing in my head over the roar of red rage. Granny Claire's voice smoothed down the fire as she whispered to my soul. *Be smart, Rose. Magick is about knowledge as much as power. There will be a time for him to hurt, but not now.*

Matthias shifted beside me, and I knew he'd heard her, too. If this was magick, it wasn't mine. At least not the magick I'd known about. This came from somewhere I'd never looked. The moment I thought it, I felt Granny smile, and it brought warmth to the ice inside me. It was a struggle, but I gained control of the rage. I looked back at the man I already knew more about than I wanted to know. But Granny was right. I didn't know what his power could do or where it came from. She had stopped him for the moment, but it would take more to put him out of the game. I gave him my best deadly glare, not a look I had perfected, but after the last few minutes, it must have worked for he nodded again.

"I don't have any more ex-husbands for you to kill, Mr. Vigil, so I think we are at what you might call a draw."

He chuckled, the congenial mask back in place. "Well done, my dear, well done."

Did he expect me to tell him you're welcome, I wondered. Was that how this game was played? I still felt icky inside from his intrusion and struggling to control my new-found violent streak. He continued to laugh as he waved off any reply I might have made.

"And you misunderstand the purpose of my invitation, my dear. This evening is for possibilities, not threats. It is for what I can offer you, not what I might take away."

From the corner of my eye, I saw the look that passed over Yvette's face. I hadn't been watching her during my *tete-a-tete* with Vigil. From what I saw on her face now, I could tell where she'd placed her bet. What she wanted to offer me held only the possibility of pain. It disappointed her for us to go back to the illusion of playing nice.

"And you have something to offer Rose, is that it?" Matthias' voice was calm. Point for him. "Besides another body for her garden?"

The pissed expression flitted over Vigil's face again. He looked at Matthias like Yvette was looking at me. Something about my chosen knight really irritated him. It made me wonder exactly what Matthias knew. *And made me think harder about who and what Matthias was.*

"Indeed I do. I have quite a lot to offer her as a matter of fact. What I wish to share with Mrs. DeSalvo will change her entire future."

"I believe you've already done that." I looked from Vigil to Eddie, who hadn't reacted to any of this so far. I was beginning to wonder if Vigil was doing something to him as well. But it could be the same old Eddie. If he wasn't the center of attention, it bored him.

Vigil waved a hand as if to dismiss Eddie's murder like old news. "I've merely interrupted it for a time. What I wish to share with you now is quite different." He glanced at Yvette. "Perhaps, my dear, you could take Edward for a walk, while my guests and I discuss the situation."

"He isn't a pet," I snapped. "And he doesn't leave my sight."

It was hard to tell, but I thought I saw a hint of relief on Yvette's face. She hadn't moved when Vigil made his command, and now she stepped back further, keeping as much distance between her and Eddie as possible.

"I can see why your husband found you a bit trying, Rosalie. Very well. We shall have our discussion with all in attendance. You may assume the responsibility for Edward's possible actions."

He spoke it like a challenge. Before I could spout something back, Matthias interrupted.

"Since I raised him, I am responsible for Eddie."

Well, didn't that put the icing on the cake. So much for my getting Matthias out of the mess. Men and their egos. They had another brief staring contest before Vigil nodded as he lowered himself into an enormous winged chair.

"This discussion is more between Mrs. DeSalvo and I. It is not really your domain. But since you appear to have ingratiated yourself with her, you are not likely to leave us alone, are you?"

"No."

I decided it was time for me to reenter the conversation. I glanced over at Eddie then gave a pointed look at the chair behind him.

"If you don't want Eddie messing up your pretty furniture, he can stand beside us."

Vigil gave me a smile that had me worried. "I think what we have to discuss would be better done when we are all comfortable. Or at least as comfortable as

Edward can get. Don't worry about the mess. Furniture can be replaced."

He motioned to Matthias and me to sit, and I started to refuse. But Matthias tugged on my hand, pulling me toward the closest chair. The thing was all velvety and cushy and looked like it might swallow me whole. Vigil probably had it trained to get rid of unpleasant guests. Matthias eased down beside me onto the arm of the chair, keeping one hand over mine like he'd hold me down if need be. Such a smart man. Eddie flopped down on what had to be the most expensive chair in the room, one he was definitely going to leave some body parts on. I shook my head. Vigil cleared his throat like he was about to give an important speech. Beside me, Matthias sat still as stone. I found myself wondering if he was a rock I could stand on or the boulder that would crush me. Guess I have some things to work out.

"What I have to tell you, dear Rosalie, is information you should have in order to make a wise choice in this affair."

"This affair? You mean my life?"

"Exactly." Vigil nodded, either oblivious to my sarcasm or unconcerned with it. "What I am offering you is the opportunity to turn from the mediocre, mundane practice you have wrapped yourself in and instead embrace your legacy. I offer you the opportunity to embrace the power you were born with."

"Since I've never seen you at any of the family reunions, I find it hard to believe you know anything about my legacy. So let's cut to the chase and talk about your deal with Eddie." I wanted to dispense with as many of the niceties as I could. If I was going to die here I didn't want a lot of chitchat beforehand.

Vigil steepled his fingers and stared at me over them. "As you wish. My deal, as you call it, was quite simple really. Your husband promised to retrieve a certain heirloom of my family's from you."

I turned to Eddie, who was pulling the velvet strings off the chair. "Retrieve it? Was that retrieval going to involve talking to me first?"

He looked up from his game of destruction and shrugged. "I was gonna take care of it."

I glared at Eddie. "You were going to rob me?"

"What? He's an antiques dealer. It's just an old cup."

"And you knew where it was?"

"It's a cup. I figured I'd walk into the kitchen and find it."

"You never walked into the kitchen the whole time we were married. For all I knew, you never even knew we had a kitchen. You ate on the couch in front of the TV for our entire married life."

"I'd've found it."

My reply was interrupted by Matthias squeezing my hand. I looked back at Vigil, who was enjoying this far too much.

"So Eddie was going to get you this heirloom and you what, got tired of waiting?"

"He failed to deliver on a contract. As a businessman, I expect to be dealt with honorably."

"Honorably? So Eddie took too long, and you killed him for it?"

The words were out before I could stop them. Matthias' fingers tightened on my wrist. He was probably regretting coming with me since it was beginning to look like I was no better at negotiating the criminal waters than Eddie had been. I wondered whose front yard we'd end up buried in.

"No. I would have much preferred a simple lesson in reliability. Though the incident caused me many complications, your husband would be a great deal better at persuading you to fulfill the commitment if he were still among the living. No, your husband's passing was his own fault."

"Ex-husband."

"Or, shall we say, the fault of his own excesses."

"Beg pardon?"

"As I began to experience some disappointment in Mr. Espinosa's services regarding my very important matter, I decided to send one of my employees to, shall we say, speed up the process. Regrettably, there was some unexplored personal history between my assistant and your husband."

"Look, it would really help if you stopped speaking in riddles. Nice as they sound, I'm not catching your drift."

"An obstacle came between your husband and Lars, my assistant."

"Did this obstacle have a name?"

"Becca, Lars' lovely young bride, who has a rather incredible appetite for...physical entanglements."

"Belinda, my ass." I glared over at Eddie, who shrugged.

I turned back to Vigil and tried to hide my disgust. "So, Eddie was banging his wife."

"A crude, but accurate interpretation of the events. When Lars recognized him as his wife's latest conquest, he lost control in the heat of the moment."

"While the knife was in his hands."

"Lars and I have had a rather in-depth discussion of the terms of his employment."

I'll bet.

"So you still want to get back whatever it was you hired Eddie to steal from me."

"I believe you have misunderstood me. Your husband was hired to speak with you on my behalf. To persuade you to return my heirloom to me. It was my understanding that your grandmother's possessions had gone to you after her death. This heirloom was one that I had given to her. I hope it does not come as too much of a shock, but your grandmother and I were, shall we say, involved, for a time. After our relationship dissolved, your grandmother decided to keep the cup, in spite of my remonstrations that it was an important part of my family lineage. Even my father was unable to persuade her to return it to our family. I am hoping you will not be so obstinate."

"So you hired Eddie. My ex-husband. A fact you should have considered. You hired Eddie for his persuasive skills? And you say you're a businessman?" I frowned at him. "Eddie and I aren't on the friendliest of terms, in case he didn't tell you. So what is this precious cup you say my grandmother kept?"

He glanced over at the ever-present Yvette, who produced an envelope I hadn't noticed her holding before. I'd gotten wrapped up in the conversation. I would make a lousy spy. Vigil dismissed her with a wave, something that did not have a pleasing effect on her countenance, before withdrawing a piece of paper and handing it to me. I stared at it for a moment before passing it to Matthias.

"This?" I frowned up at him. "This is what you're so fired up about? Some plain old cup you could get at any discount store."

I had expected gold or jewel encrusted at the very least. Something worth a great deal of money. The drawing was well-done, but the cup was simple, a bland beige, smooth and plain save for an intricate carving of some sort of city scene on one side.

Vigil took the paper from Matthias and handed it back to me. "I beg to differ. There are only three others like it in the world. Take a closer look, Mrs. DeSalvo."

I tried for my best polite stare as I gave the drawing a second look. As I stared, something about the carving on the side caught my eye. It took a moment for my brain to catch up with what my eyes were seeing, but when it did I almost dropped the paper. The carving on the cup had begun to move. Or at least the people in it had started moving. And it wasn't the happy dance, from the looks on their faces. Those looks held real fear, or as real as a carving could get. They were cowering back from something unseen, huddling together like they could hide from whatever it was. It was like one of those medieval images of sinners trapped in hell. Figures a man like Vigil would see this as something of value. Maybe he thought he could carry it around and shake it at people, and they'd be even more scared of him. I thought to tell him a gun would work better but figured he didn't need my help in his reign of terror. I didn't want anyone else to end up digging some family member out of their rose bed in the night. Point for me.

Then I noticed the longer I stared at the image, the more familiar it seemed. I thought hard for a moment and felt I heard the echo of a name somewhere in the back of my head. Hard as I tried, I couldn't grasp the name. I also couldn't shake the sense I should know something I didn't. Or maybe I did know, but didn't remember I knew.

I slid a finger across the drawing and a shiver ran down my spine. This thing knew me. The familiar feeling grew, creeping along my conscious mind with a surety I couldn't return. If it hadn't been an inanimate object, I'd swear it was calling my name. It felt all too real, like the actual cup lay beneath my fingers as I touched the paper.

I was getting too weirded out by everything. Vigil was a sicko. Maybe he had charmed the image to do something to me. I knew some magick practitioners could do that kind of thing. *And maybe I was paranoid, and he was nothing but a straightforward killer.*

As I took a deep breath to relax, hoping my face showed no emotion, my gaze caught the image again, and I sucked in a breath. The people in the carving were moving, pleading and begging for…something. Something told me if I listened hard enough I would hear their voices. Part of me wanted to drop the photo and part wanted to hold it close to my chest, to my heart. Tears welled up in my eyes, although I had no idea why. My heart ached for the moving masses, no matter how hard my brain insisted they weren't real. I needed to get away from this place, to find out what I didn't know. I was missing something, some very important piece of information I needed to have or something told me my life would never be the same again.

I felt Matthias' hand against the small of my back

as he moved up behind me to stare at the drawing. The puzzled look on his face told me he saw nothing unusual.

"Amazing."

I stared up at Vigil, hoping I'd wiped my expression clean before he saw my face. "What?"

"The cup. It reached out to you, through only an image. Pardon my excitement, Mrs. DeSalvo, but the cup was one of my family's most valued possessions. One of our most magickal possessions. Sad to say, I did not have the power to use it as it was meant to be used as a young man. I believe that now, as an older and wiser man, I will be able to unlock its full potential. It is interesting to meet someone else who may be able to say the same thing. As I said earlier, I can tell you things that will make you embrace your legacy, if you will let me. Together you and I can bring your magick into its full power. We would be a force to be reckoned with, my dear."

"Was that the kind of argument you used with her grandmother?"

There was an edge of tension in Matthias' voice. I wondered if Granny Claire was speaking to him. He locked his gaze with Vigil's, and they had another of those pissing match moments. Vigil's face looked sour when he spoke, like he'd lost the match. Or at least I hoped so.

"Claire and I were, partners, shall we say, as well as being romantically involved. She was coming to terms with her legacy, with the power that lay in her family line. Our relationship ended in a less than amicable manner. Claire kept the cup out of spite, I believe."

I could no more imagine my granny involved with this man than I could see pigs flying. There was nothing about him that would have attracted the woman I knew.

"Then you didn't know my grandmother at all. She never did anything out of spite."

"I would not disrespect your memory of her, my dear, but our relationship was of a different kind than yours. The kind that often ends in spite when it's over."

"Whatever. It seems most of your relationships don't end well." I glanced at Eddie then started to hand the paper back to Vigil. Instead of taking it, he waved a hand at me.

"Keep it. You'll need it to find the cup for me."

He emphasized the last part as if it were a reminder. Or a message. There was no mistaking the threat behind the words. I folded the paper and shoved it in my pocket. Something still nagged at me, but I wasn't sure exactly what. I looked up at Vigil.

"So why didn't you get the cup back from my parents after my grandmother passed? If it were truly yours, you could have simply asked for it back."

"I was, regrettably, out of the country when your grandmother passed away. I had business interests needing attention. I've only recently returned to my home."

"You've been gone for twelve years, and the first thing you want to do when you get back is find an old cup?"

"I believe you've noticed, Mrs. DeSalvo, the object in question is hardly an old cup, as you put it. Its value far exceeds anything you can imagine. Its value to you, as well, as to me."

"Yeah, you keep talking about my legacy. And I'm

assuming that legacy involves this cup. A cup you want me to give back because it belongs to your family, to you. As I said before, I don't think you and I share any family ties, none that I know of anyway. So what does my family's supposed legacy have to do with this cup?"

"Do you believe in a world beyond this one, Mrs. DeSalvo?"

"You mean do I believe in heaven?"

He rolled his eyes. "A trite concept designed to quiet the fears of children. What I am speaking of is far more impressive than harps and angels on clouds. Far more powerful. Help me in my quest, and I shall show you wonders you have never imagined."

"So my great legacy is to be your sidekick. I give you back this powerful artifact you say is yours, in spite of the fact that it was in my grandmother's possession, and agree to help you find wonders beyond my imagination. Wonders I suppose aren't going to be mine. Doesn't sound so amazing, Vigil. Sounds kind of like my legacy isn't worth spit."

Beside me Eddie snorted. I didn't hear anything from Matthias, but his grip on my hand got a bit tighter. I looked from Vigil to Eddie and back.

"Right now I'd say I have other things to deal with that are a bit more important to my future than being a pawn in your discovering your great power. Solving them just might keep me out of jail for murder. That sounds like a better legacy to me."

"I would have thought you would have learned your lesson in regards to your husband by now, dear Rosalie."

The mask fell back off, leaving the real monster staring at me again as he moved toward me. Behind me

I thought I heard Eddie whimper. Matthias' face froze into that cold stillness I realized was a clear sign of his power rising. Vigil stopped about an inch out of my personal comfort zone.

"Whether or not you choose to partner with me in my endeavors is not the most important point I am trying to make. The cup is mine. I will have it, make no mistake about it. Your husband failed me, and I believe the consequences make my intentions quite clear."

I held my breath as I tried to still the shaking inside me. "I will look for your cup."

"I wouldn't take too long." Yvette nodded toward Eddie, who sat picking scabs off his forearms. "I'm no expert in your so-called magick, but I would say your time is limited." The expression on her face told me she'd like to see it run out real soon.

"Mr. Vigil, it would be much easier if you told me somewhere, um, that I could lay Eddie to rest so I can have time to look instead of chasing him everywhere or trying to hide him." I thought I sounded reasonable. At least reasonable was what I was going for.

Vigil turned to pour himself a glass of wine from the decanter on the pretty cherry table. The mask was back in place when he faced me again. As he lifted the delicate crystal to his lips he smiled.

"I'm sure it would make things easier on you, however, the ease of the task is not my concern. Easiest would have been for your husband to deliver on his promise in the first place. Since you appear to have no desire to uncover your own power through my tutelage, I feel we have no other business beyond the return of the cup. Until such time as it is returned to me, Edward stays above ground. It will give you added incentive to complete your task and keep you from going to the authorities with anything you become privy to regarding me or my business interests."

"So Eddie's insurance?" Matthias glanced from Eddie to Vigil.

"Precisely, Mr. Romero. Once the job is complete, I will be happy to provide a resting place for Edward where he will remain undetected for many years. Until that time, his presence is your problem."

Chapter Ten

We drove aimlessly around after leaving Vigil's. None of us had much to say, not even Eddie. Especially not Eddie. He hadn't met my eyes since we got back in the car. But then I kept my gaze directed out the window, at a world that suddenly seemed very dangerous.

"Rose."

Matthias glanced over at me, and I started trembling.

"No, don't talk. Can't you feel it? The calm, the stillness. It's like we're in a little bubble, floating along on the breeze, away from everything."

"Rose—"

"Uh-uh. You talk and that bubble's gonna burst. Then we'll be right back in the middle of the bad shit. I don't want to be right back in the middle of the bad shit."

"News flash, we're still in the middle of the bad shit. It's all around us."

"Well then we're screwed." I looked over at him. "Or at least I'm screwed. You can walk away."

Matthias whipped the car over to the side of the road and slammed it in park so fast I got whiplash. I looked over at him. His hands gripped the steering wheel. The look on his face told me he was probably counting to ten. At least ten. Behind me, Eddie straightened himself up off the floor where he had slid.

"That's probably not good for your engine." I said it with a nervous laugh, anything to lighten the mood. Humor is one of my strong points.

He leaned over, gripped me by the shoulders and dragged me right up in his face.

"Nobody's walking anywhere. I didn't come into this on a whim, and I'm not leaving till it's over. And I do plan on being able to leave, on being very much alive when this is done. In spite of my gifts, I don't have a death wish. So stop whining, and start thinking about what you're going to do."

I shoved him back, which took a bit more strength than I'd planned on. "Why did you come into this? What was all that posturing between you and Vigil?"

"Not important now. No more distractions. No more pretense. Start talking, Rose."

I stared at the man breathing fire in my direction then looked out the window.

"This sounds like it's going to be a one-sided conversation, and I don't like sitting on the side of the road. Let's wait until we're—"

"Until we're what? Back home? Back where you're safe and you don't have to deal with who you are or what you are? Uh-uh. Here. Now. Start talking."

"About what? About how scared I am? About how I don't have a clue what's going on? Can you tell me something that will fix that?"

He looked away.

"Yeah, that's what I thought. You and Vigil both keep talking about who I am. What do you mean, who I am? Clearly it's something different than what I'm thinking. You say it like you know what I don't. I told you who I was before you agreed to come out and play tonight. If you're under some sort of delusion that there's more to it than that, you need to get over it. And if you're trying to spur me on to being something else then you're in for a disappointment. I'm tired of being insulted by people who seem to think that what I am isn't good enough."

He must have made it to the number ten, because when he spoke again his voice was back to its usual calm.

"Rose, people are dead. Threats are being made. We just spent an hour trading chitchat with a killer. Don't you think it's time to start taking your gift seriously?"

"Just because there are some things I choose not to pursue—"

"None of us can afford your choice. Nor can we afford for you to walk away from the truth."

"And what if I don't have what it takes to use this gift you keep talking about? Huh, what about that? What about how badly I could mess up if it turns out I'm not as gifted as you think?"

I squeezed my eyes shut to keep the tears from falling. Matthias leaned close to me, lifting one hand to my cheek. His finger traced the tear that escaped, smoothing the dampness of it across my skin before coming back to cup my chin. I opened my eyes, staring into a face that scared the hell out of me. Too handsome, too able to see into my soul, and there was too much knowledge in his dark eyes. As I stared, he leaned over and planted a careful kiss on my lips. The heat of him lingered on my skin after he moved back. Now I was really scared, because I knew I could get used to feeling that heat.

"And what if you are as gifted as I think, Rose, or even more so. How will you ever know if you don't try? If you don't ever let yourself find out, then you're sure to never know. And everyone else will suffer." I tried not to flinch at what I saw in his eyes. "How many people do you have to find buried in your yard before you grow up?"

"Don't lay this guilt trip on me." My voice sounded whiny even to me. "I'm having enough of one without your help."

"A guilt trip over not being who you are?"

"Over not wanting to be…that." The fight went out of me as the words echoed in the car. "Because learning all this means…certain things."

"Certain things?"

"It means that IT is real."

"It?"

"IT. The thing. The most important part of all of it, of who I am and what I was supposed to do here, to do with my life. It means I'm not imagining all those dreams, all the extra things that come at me from the edges, things that I don't really understand. Things that scare the shit out of me."

"Ah. And now shit's getting real. About damn time." Matthias glanced back at Eddie. "Ready for it or not, Rose, real has arrived. It's sitting in the back seat grunting. You'd best be thinking about what you're going to do. And that needs to include all the options, and knowing all the power on our side."

"Do?" I wanted to cry so I yelled instead. "I can't do any of this. I so can't do this."

"And what do you think your options are?"

"How the hell would I know? This is your game, not mine. You can shake me, yell at me or kiss me senseless, it isn't going to help. Nothing can help. I don't do this kind of thing. That's the bottom line."

He stared at me hard, and I felt it all the way down to my bones. Dear Goddess, I thought, if he uses that voice on me I'm toast.

"You may not have done this kind of thing before, Rose, but you damn well better be ready to do it now."

He combined the voice with the stare, and it stopped the smartass comeback forming in my brain.

"That is, if you like living. And since I plan on living, you'd better plan on living through this, too. What the hell did you think would happen when you called me in the middle of the night?"

"I don't know! Did it look to you like my brain was working in high gear when you got to my house? I'd spent the last hour digging my ex-husband out of my flower bed and hoping the neighbors didn't see. That's as far as my thinking skills got me. If Mama hadn't known about you, I'd still be pacing around that tarp, wondering if I could fit Eddie into a bag of potting soil. In case you haven't noticed, I'm not much of a planner. Especially when it comes to this."

"This?"

I was already tired of our talk so I clamped my lips shut. What I really wanted was comfort. Or another hot kiss. One look at Matthias' face told me I probably wasn't getting another one of those. He gripped my chin in his hand and spoke clearly and calmly through his clenched teeth.

"There are some objects, some powerful objects, things that many people would kill to possess."

I jerked away from him. "Like this magickal cup Vigil wants. Yeah, I get that. Vigil certainly isn't above killing. Eddie's proof of that. And we're probably next on the list if I don't get him this cup."

"And what happens if you give him the cup?"

That made my stomach bottom out. In all my fear I hadn't really thought about that. The image of the moving people came back and so did the chill. What were they asking of me, those carved faces that had pleaded for something from me, something I didn't understand.

"I don't know. I guess he gets to plant more people under rose bushes."

Matthias shook his head. "Don't count on it being that easy."

I knew he was right. "So you're saying that even if he gets the cup, we could be the ones who get planted under the rosebushes this time."

"That's a definite possibility."

"Is there really a choice here? You're saying I need to know what the cup is. But knowing isn't going to change the fact that Vigil wants it, and will do whatever he has to do to get his hands on it."

"Knowing what the cup is could change the balance of power in this situation."

"So you're ruling out the option where not knowing gets us out of this whole situation?"

He nodded. "Knowledge is power, Rose, never forget that. What you know, you can handle. It's the unknown you have to worry about."

"So the next step is to find the cup."

"Do you remember it?"

I started to shake my head then stopped. Something

about it was familiar, even though I would have sworn I'd never seen it. I glanced behind me at Eddie, who was staring off into space, grunting now and then.

"How much time do we have to do this?"

Matthias followed my gaze. "Not long."

"Vigil's never going to just let us put Eddie back into the ground and walk away, is he?"

"No."

"You really don't know how to comfort a girl, do you?"

He looked startled for a minute then he laughed. "I do. As soon as we're out of this I'll show you some things. I don't know how comforting they'll be, but I can promise you'll enjoy them."

I'll bet.

He pulled back from me. "But for now, I don't want you comforted. I don't want you complacent. I want you anxious. And I want you angry."

"Angry I can do. As a matter of fact, I was surprised to find that on my plate, smooshed there among the scared shitless and in way over my head feelings."

"It shouldn't come as a surprise, Rose." He glanced over at me. "I want you to think about something else."

"Okay." I said it slow and with the suspicion I felt. Something about the look on his face told me I wasn't going to like his next words.

"I want you to think about the power inside you." He lifted a hand to forestall my protest. "It isn't just a want, Rose, it's a need. You need to know more. You need to know why, you need to know how, you need to know all those things you've kept yourself from knowing until now. You need to. We need you to."

Well, when he put it like that. I sighed.

"There isn't anything to know. I don't know what this cup is. I don't know where it is. If Granny had it, I never saw it."

As the words came out of my mouth, I had another inkling of doubt. My small voice was whispering that I was wrong. I wished it would whisper the location and the meaning of it all, but it stuck with me being wrong.

Matthias gave me another of those looks that didn't soothe me. "There's something else you need to realize, Rose."

"What?"

"That things aren't always what they seem. That people aren't always who, or what they seem."

"You mean like my grandmother being…involved with Vigil." It was hard to even get the words out. They left a nasty taste in my mouth.

"I mean the possibility that what Vigil told you isn't the truth."

"You mean on top of being a cold-blooded killer, the man is also a liar? Wow, that thought never occurred to me."

"Just because he tells you he gave the cup to your grandmother when they were romantically involved doesn't make that the way things really happened."

"It doesn't make it not true either. Maybe that's the worst part of trying to do this."

"What is?"

I shook my head. "I don't know who anyone is." I looked at him and made my voice as careful as I could. "I don't know who you are."

"I'm a friend, Rose. Whatever else you have doubts about, know that I'm on your side."

"I have a side?" I leaned my head against the window and closed my eyes. "Sides mean there are winners and losers. Can't we all just come together?"

"Peace, love and unity are not the operative words here."

"I just wanted to help, you know? A love charm for geeky Alan Bradford, so Nova Hammond would give him a second look. Herbs for Mrs. Carvey, so her arthritis would be more bearable. Doing an astrology chart now and then. Stuff like that. That's all I wanted. I liked doing that. Not this. Never this."

"And harm none, huh?"

I laughed. "Yeah, that's the part I really liked. Mama tells me it's because I'm basically a busybody, but I want to help, I like to help."

"You don't see this as helping?"

"Uh-uh. I can see major hurt down this path. This isn't what I wanted."

"And that's why you've stayed so carefully mediocre."

"What?" I frowned at him. "What do you mean?"

"Come on, Rose. Alexis would not have stuck with you for three years if you were as bad at magick as you make out. I know her, she's not that nice."

"I have made some progress, but this...no, it isn't me. I know herbs, the elements, astrological signs. I help people figure out how to harness the energy around them to move their life along. I don't raise the dead."

At that Matthias raised an eyebrow.

"Okay, so you raised the dead, but I mean, it's not something I even watch normally. I don't run around in the night meeting with bad guys. I don't battle sorcerers for magickal objects. I don't have formulas in my head for spells to control magickal objects."

"For someone who wants to help harness positive energy, you've got a lot of negativity going there."

"What?"

He shrugged. "All I heard in all that was a whole lot of don'ts. Negative."

"You asked. I'm just telling you I don't do this kind of thing."

"You push the thought away, yet you have dabbled in some of this, as you call it."

I gazed up at him, and he nodded.

"You wanted to know about me. Well, I needed to know a little bit about you, too. One of the reasons I agreed to come to your house was curiosity."

"How? Who?"

"I called Alexis after I hung up the phone with you. Come on, Rose, you don't expect me to rush over to the home of every crazy woman who calls me in the middle of the night wanting a dead ex-husband raised. I did a bit of checking before I put myself in the middle of something that might end up being rather sticky."

"And has ended up that way."

He nodded. "You know, it's time you started telling yourself the truth. If all you wanted to do was help people, why not go to nursing school instead?"

"I can't stand the sight of blood. Makes me want to throw up."

Matthias stared at me for a moment then the laughter rolled out of him. He laughed and laughed while I glared at him. I probably could've kept the glare going if I hadn't caught sight of Eddie out of the corner of my eye. The laughter bubbled out of me as I watched what was left of the man who had once been the man of my dreams make fog faces on the window as if he hadn't a care in the world. I guess he didn't really. He'd already left this world so what was left to hurt him. My small voice told me I didn't want to know the answer to that question.

Chapter Eleven

"So what do we do now?"

I glanced over at Matthias, hoping he had at least an idea of what should happen next. If he didn't we were really screwed. We'd finally gotten ourselves under control and back on the road. Part of me wanted to run back home and put my head under the covers. The realization that Eddie would be sitting there staring at me while I did put a damper on the pleasure of that plan.

"We find the cup."

"Sounds simple." I rolled my eyes.

"Use your senses, Rose. If the cup belonged to your grandmother, then you can trace it back through her things. Alexis says you're good at creating spells on the fly. Use your magick."

I laughed. "Alexis told you that, huh? It still amazes me she would admit I'm good at anything. I didn't think she told anybody about the agreement she made to mentor me. It doesn't seem one of her most enjoyable experiences."

"Alexis enjoys everything she does, or she doesn't do it. If she's continuing to mentor you, it means she believes you have potential. Maybe that's something you should think about."

His face carried that eerie stillness as he looked at me. It wasn't only his voice that could pull things out of you. I felt a deep yearning inside me, like I was waiting for something I'd longed for all my life. If I could only figure out what it was.

"But we'll get back to that later."

My inner child did the happy dance, thankful Matthias was willing to shift the conversation. Right now, I was pretty sure I couldn't make it through another lecture. And I sure as hell didn't want to think about whether or not my avoidance had been a grave mistake.

"For now," he continued, "let me explain. All magick leaves a trail, even hidden magick."

"Because magick is energy and energy can be felt."

He smiled at me like I'd gone to the head of the class. "Exactly. If Vigil is certain you can find the cup, then for some reason he feels the energy of the cup's magick links to you."

"Or to my grandmother. He must have given her the cup for a reason."

"If he did indeed give it to her."

"You think he didn't? Do you think she stole it?"

The idea horrified me. It wasn't something I could associate with the woman I knew at all.

"Maybe she's not the thief."

I looked at Matthias. "But he said she had it. And he clearly doesn't have it, or he wouldn't be going around throwing dead bodies in people's yards to find it."

"I'll agree he doesn't have it. But I think we need to be very careful about everything else he's said. We need to keep in mind that he wants it, and he's not a man who would worry about how he got it."

"Boy, there is nothing easy about this, is there."

He shook his head. "No. I don't think anything that happens this night is going to be easy. Let's go back to your house. There we can start looking. We also need to know about Vigil's people."

"Well, Yvette's no worry, not from the magickal standpoint. All she's got going for her are D-cups and stilettos." I looked away as I realized how bitchy that must have come off. "At least from what I could tell," I added lamely.

He grinned. "You picked up on her easy enough."

I snorted this time. "Because she pissed me off. She didn't scare the shit out of me. I've dealt with her kind all my life."

"Exactly. That battle is familiar territory."

"But if it's true that I have some deep, innate power I haven't tapped into yet, then you'd think Vigil'd be a bit scared of me. Or at least cautious about pissing me off. And I didn't pick up on that one bit."

"Not if he can keep you more scared of him. And, as I said, many people, especially powerful people like Vigil who are used to buying what they want or frightening people into giving it to them, don't always understand the terms certain artifacts work under. Even having powerful magick inside them doesn't guarantee they have knowledge as well. Magick craves power, but those who wield it don't always understand the role knowledge plays in acquiring that power. They don't understand that acquiring power is as much training and study as it is wielding and using."

"Or scaring and threatening." I bumped my head back against the seat and closed my eyes. "Training and study, huh? I think I'm kind of lacking in that department."

"Not according to Alexis."

I frowned up at him. "Are you serious?"

"She's given you the knowledge. What you've lacked is the motivation to use it. Tonight that changed."

I had to agree with him. I looked in the rearview mirror at my motivation as he sat in the back, trying to wrap his loose skin back around his arm. Tonight had made me way motivated to do whatever it took to get back to my life. My only hope was that I'd survive tonight, motivation or not.

"You're a witch, Rose. You've got the skill, you've had the training. You've just never let it be a part of you, a part of who you are. It's time to tap into the magick that's always been inside you. Think of this as your final exam."

I laughed. "A part of me, huh? I think I may be about to flunk my final exam if that's the case."

"How about we grab something to eat and energize ourselves so you can cram for the test?"

Food sounded wonderful. We headed through the closest drive-thru burger joint. I was so focused on what I wanted to eat that for a moment I didn't see the horrified look on the face of the girl at the window. She was staring into the car like she was watching a train wreck—a terrible sight, but she couldn't look away. I glanced around behind me in time to catch Eddie giving her a wink. The gashes on his face were translucent in the neon light, making his unhealthy green glow shine in the dark. A flap of skin fell over one eyebrow and a thick crust of blood had settled on his chin. He puckered up his lips to blow her a kiss just as his gaze caught me staring at him.

"Eddie!" I hissed as I slapped Matthias' arm to get his attention. He turned to Eddie and frowned.

"What?" Eddie gave me that look that he used when he wanted to appear at his most innocent. Only in his present condition, it pulled his rubbery face into a grimace that made him ten times scarier.

"He's going to get us arrested."

"I know that." I grumbled. "You're the expert here. What do you want me to do about it?"

Matthias glanced over at the girl, who'd shut the glass window but still peered through it.

"Tell her something."

"Tell her what? I hated to leave him home alone, poor guy, being dead and all. He is my ex-husband. No sense in treating him nasty. Do you think that might calm her down?

"Being a smartass isn't helpful." I managed not to stick my tongue out at him. Eddie leaned forward and opened his mouth, like he wanted to yell something to the girl out the window. I reached back and clamped a hand over his mouth then immediately regretted it. His lips were cold and clammy and something oozed over my hand. I shoved him further into the back seat. It was a good thing he had on a thick sweatshirt because my hand went through his chest.

"Sit back and behave, Eddie. You're making things worse, as usual."

"She's looking at us again." Matthias motioned to the girl at the window, who held our bag of food in one hand, the other hand on the window. Guess she was trying to get up the courage to open it. "Tell her he's got some sort of, I don't know, something wrong with him."

"Well, duh. Now that's a much better option."

"We don't have time for sarcasm. This is your area of expertise. I'll hold up my end with the skills I've got, and you've got to do the same. Have you got enough skill with glamour to get by her at least long enough to get us out of here?"

He was right, and I knew it. I'd dragged him into all this with my wild phone call in the middle of the night, and now I needed to start holding up my end of this bargain. Alexis and I had spent an entire month on the basics of using glamour. She'd started with little things, like using it to flirt in bars. Nothing that covered trying to convince a terrified girl that she didn't really see the walking dead man in front of her. But from the way Matthias was glaring at me, I thought I'd better at least try.

"I'll give it a shot." I pasted on my best fake smile as the girl finally got the courage to shove the bag out the little window. It took a bit of concentration to focus on her while chanting the words Alexis had taught me over and over in my head. That's my only excuse for the pitiful reason I gave her.

"I'm sorry." I smiled at her as Matthias took the bag. She avoided touching him or making eye contact with any of us. I couldn't see her other hand, but wondered if it was resting on a phone, just waiting for us to drive off so she could dial 911. I leaned across Matthias to get closer to her to whisper.

"We've tried not to make a big deal about it, I mean, he really likes to get out of the house every once in a while. So we don't mention the way, you know, he looks, 'cause it would make him self-conscious."

The subject of all my apparent tender loving care

leaned his face against the window and puckered his lips at her. Matthias reached back and gave him a shove. I focused more of my attention on her face, trying to put as much energy as I could into the spell.

"My friend has a skin disorder. I guess that's obvious, huh?"

"A skin disorder?" She seemed torn between looking at Eddie and looking at me. I spoke low, so she'd have to get close to hear me. I wanted all of her focus on me.

"Yeah. He's got, um, eczema."

"Eczema?"

"Yeah. He's got it bad. Really bad eczema. But the doctor says it's treatable. It's just going to take a while."

"He's got eczema."

There was less of a question in her voice this time, and I felt her slipping just a bit into my words. I pumped up the energy into the spell, putting as much hypnotic input as I could into my voice.

"I appreciate you being so friendly to him. It helps him to get out every once in a while. It's good for his socialization."

She turned a blank stare to me. "Yeah, no problem. They train us good on customer service here."

I waved at her as we drove off.

"Eczema?"

I ignored the sarcasm in Matthias' voice and smiled to myself. I'd just glamoured a total stranger. Things were looking up.

Chapter Twelve

"Coffee break?"

Matthias stood in the doorway. After we'd eaten, he'd said he had some calls to make. I think he recognized that I needed a few minutes to collect myself before we headed up to the attic where Granny Claire's things were stored. I still hadn't thrown up in front of him, and I wanted to keep it that way. Now that I had food in my stomach, that might take some extra effort.

I also needed a bit of distance between us because I still couldn't stifle the urge to rub up against him. Alexis taught me that sex is a great way to ground excess energy and boy, was I feeling a lot of excess energy right now. Keeping my distance might keep me from embarrassing myself by crawling all over him. I had to keep reminding myself the reason he was here. It wasn't like we'd met under opportune circumstances. So I'd headed to the kitchen to make coffee. Probably not the best option for my nerves, but sitting there staring at the photo Vigil had given me wasn't helping either.

"Just need a little stimulation." I kept my gaze focused on the coffeemaker and off the man I wanted to lick all over. *What was wrong with me? Sex shouldn't be on my mind in the middle of the worst day of my life.* Although, all the other options of what should be on my mind didn't hold much appeal. "Did you finish your phone calls?"

Matthias moved up behind me, throwing a monkey wrench into my plan for distance. He reached past me for a cup, putting all that heat and muscled flesh in front of me like a red flag. I froze where I stood. *Don't make eye contact, don't make eye contact.*

"Waiting for one to call me back. I'd think the events of the last few hours had provided enough stimulation for a few days, maybe even a few weeks."

He backed up, cup in hand, and I started to breathe again. That might have been a mistake, because the scent of him filtered across every nerve ending within my body.

"Guess I needed a little bit of normal. Thought I'd make coffee and take a break from living dangerously for a few minutes." I turned and gave him my best perky smile.

"There's something to be said for living dangerously, Rose. Maybe that's one of the changes you need to make."

He whispered the words against my skin seconds before he pressed his lips to mine. All my resolve vanished as I sank into him with the sensation of need like nothing I'd felt before. He was hot and hard. Touching him almost exploded my danger meter. Power of a different kind wrapped around me, ancient and primal and full of volatile things like lust and desire, sex and need. With a groan he wrapped his arms around my waist, pulling me in against him so close I felt his heart pound against my own.

I melted into his body as if I could go through skin and bone all the way to pleasure. I think I might have made one of those embarrassing sounds, something between a groan and a sob. He had one leg between mine, his knee pressed against a part of my anatomy that longed to do some exploring. I rubbed myself along his jeans, like I'd wanted to since I first saw him stalking across my front yard. In the back of my mind, I had the thought to strip off my clothes and his too so I could feel more of the heat radiating off him, but then I realized there was background music. Very unromantic background music. It was the theme song from the Addams Family. Matthias made a sound of his own as he pulled his cell from his pocket. Nice to know I wasn't the only one caught up in the moment. He held the phone down against his leg for a minute while those dark eyes stared at me. Having him look at me like that didn't help me get my heart rate down.

"Think about it, Rose." He stalked out of the kitchen as he answered the call.

I doubted I'd be thinking about much else, at least not until I got my breathing back under control. Watching his ass as he walked through the door didn't help with that at all. Wow.

"So, is he a good kisser?"

Startled, I turned to find Eddie standing in the doorway.

"I am not discussing my love life with you, Eddie."

I sat down at the table. As I watched Eddie stumble to the chair next to me, I realized he'd probably spent more time in the kitchen in the last few hours than he did the whole time we were married. Funny what stands out to you when you're losing your mind.

"Just asking. Don't get huffy."

I sighed. "You're my ex-husband, with the

emphasis on the ex. Not that I have a love life to discuss." *Did I? Could you call a couple of kisses a love life?*

"But you like him?"

"I told you, I am not going to discuss this with you." I started to get up, and he put out a hand to touch me. I stared at him. His fingers stopped a fraction of an inch from my arm.

"We had a good fire once."

"Eddie, you were stoking too many fires to have kept ours going. Let it go. I did, a long time ago."

"Okay, okay." He held up both hands. "I cheated. You never let me forget it."

"I was trying to remind you of your wedding vow, you jerk, not how many times you broke it. Once was enough."

I was surprised to find a lump in my throat at the memory of those nights, of the times he came home smelling of some other woman's perfume or her hair stuff.

"What are you trying to do here, Eddie, make me remember I swore off men 'cause they lie and cheat?"

"I'm not trying to mess things up with him. I can't compete, that's for damn sure."

Okay, I shouldn't still be a sucker for the hurt look in his eyes. Eddie could conjure that look better and quicker than any spell I could work. He shoved his hands in the front pocket of the jacket and winced.

"Are you okay?"

"Don't worry, I'm not going to fall apart here on your kitchen floor."

"Look, Eddie, I'm sorry." I sat back down and tried to think of a way to comfort him that didn't involve touching. "We're all tired and grouchy and a little out of sorts."

"Some of us are dead."

"And some of us are dead. Eddie, you know I'm sorry you're dead. It wasn't what I wanted to happen to you."

"Told everybody I should get run over by a semi, I should be shot by some husband, something heavy should fall on me while I'm napping in the truck—"

"All right, Eddie, I was angry, okay? I wanted you to hurt. I didn't really want you dead. If you died then I couldn't keep plotting your death over and over again." I rested my forehead on the table. There seemed to be no end to the curve my life had taken tonight.

"Like I made you hurt."

"What?" I lifted my face and stared at him. In all the time we were married and ever since the divorce I had never known Eddie to make any admission of guilt, to talk of any role he played in the brutal demise of our short-lived marriage. "What did you say?"

"I hurt you, okay, I know that."

"Wow, I can't tell you how good it is to hear that come out of your mouth."

"Figured. I know I never said I was sorry. But I thought, hell, she already thinks I'm sorry, no point saying it."

"And that statement sums up so much of what went wrong between us, Eddie."

"What, I should've groveled, should've said I'm an asshole?"

"It was just easier to let me blame myself, to let me go on thinking, and hearing from your darling mother, how I didn't measure up and that's why you didn't come home at night."

"You never liked my mother, never cared about what she said."

"Yes, I did, Eddie, at least at first. I was a kid, stupid and terrified and bullied by the woman you put on such a pedestal."

"You were so freaking intense."

"I was in love, Eddie. Young girls in love are intense."

"You scared the shit out of me most of the time."

"So add another thing to the million ways it was my fault. What else is new?"

"Fuck, same as always. You don't hear me, just barrel over me. Even now I'm dead."

"I told you I was tired. I'm sorry but…"

"It wasn't that you didn't cook like my mama or you were so anal you could drive a sane man to drink, which you are by the way."

I glared at him.

"Wasn't you, Rose. Just wasn't me either."

"Eddie, that makes no sense. It wasn't either of us? Who the hell else was part of the marriage?"

"That's just it. Marriage wasn't me."

"That's it?"

"That's it. I couldn't do it." I opened my mouth, and he shook his head. "Okay, okay, I didn't want to do it. Not like you wanted."

"How many ways are there to be married?"

He shrugged. "You would've never been happy with me, Rose. Hell, you weren't happy with me on our wedding day."

"Of course I wasn't. You got drunk as a skunk and hit on my cousin from Dothan."

"She was your cousin?"

"Eddie…"

"Okay. We couldn't have done it, not for long. This guy, maybe."

"Matthias?"

"He's like you, intense. Weird-ass vibes coming off him, just like you."

"Weird vibes?"

"Yeah." Eddie shuddered. "I'd feel you even when you weren't in the room. You gave off…this glow, laying there in the bed asleep. Like you were a ghost or something."

"I glowed?"

He ignored me as he stumbled up from the chair. He took a couple of shuffling steps away from me before turning back. And he looked scared.

"Worst was those times when you went places."

"When I went places?"

"Yeah. One minute asleep beside me and the next…gone somewhere else. Not sleeping but not awake either."

I stared at him dumbfounded. I had never experimented with trance journeys or astral travel. For some reason I'd never wanted to explore, that was a part of magick I wanted nothing to do with. And I sure wouldn't have experimented in my sleep. I shook my head.

"Eddie, I don't know what you're talking about. I never went anywhere in my sleep."

He gave me a thoughtful look. It was an expression I'd never seen on his face, and it gave me pause.

"Yeah, you did, Rose. Maybe I don't know you, but you don't know you either. You got no idea how scary what's inside you can be for somebody as ordinary as me."

With that pronouncement, he shuffled toward the door.

"Where are you going?" I had visions of him heading to one of his ex-girlfriends just like he always had after we'd had an argument.

"Out to the greenhouse." He gave me a sad look. "Think we'll all be more comfortable if I'm out there."

I didn't know if I believed any of us were ever going to be comfortable again, but I didn't argue with him.

Chapter Thirteen

"It's the only thing I know of that might help."

I held the old metal key tight in my hand and stared at the scarred wood door. This was a moment I had put off for almost twelve years and to tell the truth, I'd prefer to put it off for at least another twenty. But Matthias was standing beside me, and I figured he wasn't willing to wait that long. Since I couldn't get him to abandon ship, I guess I was obligated to do this tonight.

"The day after my grandmother's funeral I helped my mother bring Granny Claire's things up to this attic. I remember it clearly, and there was no cup like that one in any of her stuff. That much I'm sure of."

"But you remember this letter she left you."

I nodded. "In her Book of Shadows, there was an envelope with my name on it. And underneath my name she'd written the word important in big letters. I never opened it. I just couldn't. After that night I didn't...I just didn't want to read it."

"Rose."

"I know. I can't hide anymore."

I put the key in the lock and turned. The door swung open with more ease than I expected after so many years. The old chest stood in the same spot, the early morning light casting a glow that made a halo around it. How many times had I knelt beside it as

Granny put away her ritual tools or pulled out what she needed for her spells? Everything in there had seemed magickal to me then. It was part of her and so was I. At least that's what she used to tell me. I wondered now what she'd been trying to say that she'd never been able to find the right words for. Or the right time for. As I lifted the lid, I was both comforted and confused by the rich earthy scent wafting out of the trunk. Granny Claire's scent. As a kid it always made me feel happy, secure. Sniffing it let me know she was there, by my side.

I still am.

I closed my eyes as I felt her love wash over me.

"These are her things?"

Matthias' deep voice behind me made me grip the lid tighter. I was in over my head, and I knew it. This man wielded a power greater than any I'd ever been around, walked in a world light years from the one I inhabited. *Was that the attraction Granny felt for Vigil? Was I falling into the same trap?*

I heard the thunk of his boots as he crossed the room. My hands kept digging, digging into Granny Claire's trunk, pushing what had been so precious aside in a rush to prove…to prove what? That I didn't own a magickal cup, that none of this night had happened. That I was exactly who I said I was. He knelt beside me.

"Remember what I said earlier."

"What?" I blinked up at him, shutting off the tears as best I could.

"Just because Vigil said it doesn't make it true. He has an agenda. He will do or say whatever he thinks will get him what he wants. Keep that in mind."

"What could she have seen in him if it wasn't the magick?"

I sank down to the floor and folded my arms around myself. It took all I had not to start rocking and moaning. The ache pressed against my heart as if it would rupture it. Maybe it already had and that's why it hurt so bad.

Matthias knelt down and gripped my arms, giving me a shake. "Stop it, Rose. You don't have time for this. Listen to me. Nothing is true until you know it's true. Got it?"

I nodded. "Got it."

"You've been running from what you are. Today that changes. But you have to understand that not all who inherit the power run from it. Your grandmother didn't. She accepted who she was. That put her in a place where she faced people like Vigil. Being in that place doesn't make her bad, it makes her real. Magick is a gift and, used wisely, a benefit. And it's also a responsibility. One you can no longer run from."

I snorted. "You say that like it's so easy."

"Not easy. But possible."

I turned back to the wood chest. "Possible, huh? It's always possible, sport, that I'm really not as gifted as you think. Maybe I'm the defective part of the family. Maybe that's why my grandmother never told me any of this, because she knew I couldn't handle it. That I didn't have what it took to handle it."

He shrugged. "Then we die. At least you won't have to worry about reburying Eddie."

I frowned. "Well, isn't that comforting."

"It's the best I've got. If you're going to wallow in mediocrity, I'm not responsible for waxing poetic about it. Eddie didn't die because of who your grandmother was. He died because of who you are, because of what you possess. He died because of what Vigil wants to take from you today, right here, right now. That's what you need to focus on."

He leaned down and wiped a tear from my face.

"Now, let's find that letter and see what it can tell us. Then we'll see if you're up to this or not."

I reached down to the bottom where I'd watched my mom place Granny's Book of Shadows. Maybe she thought if she put it as deep down as she could I wouldn't come find it again. My mother had a lot of issues with the Craft. Not like Aunt Anya, but things she held against her own mother from her childhood. Fears, mostly. Guess she and I were a lot alike in that respect. As I pulled the thick volume out of the chest, power hummed along the faded leather cover. It tingled across my skin as a memory ran across my mind, something unpleasant and all too real. No matter how much I wanted to ignore it, the power left no doubt in my mind that it was time to remember, time to acknowledge I had indeed seen the cup before. I'd seen it and touched it the night Granny Claire died.

"What is it, Rose?"

I looked up at him, unable to open my mouth for fear of the pain that would leap out if I did. Something in my eyes must have reached him, for he took my hand and squeezed it.

"Take a deep breath, Rose, and let it come. Just let it come and everything will be all right."

I shook my head. I knew I didn't want that memory to come clear to me, that if it did I'd feel something I'd walled off a long time ago. And everything would be far from all right if that happened.

"To know is better." Matthias gripped my hand tighter when I started to pull away. "You can handle what you know. Fear lives in the unknown, Rose."

"Do you remember that night?"

Startled by the sound of Eddie's voice, I turned to find him standing in the doorway. He looked at me with that same peculiar look he'd had in the kitchen.

"What?" I tried to decipher the look on Eddie's face. There was a concern there I had never seen before. "Of course I remember that night."

"You talk about it in your sleep."

Now I knew I talked in my sleep. Hell, I'd woken myself up a couple of times talking in my sleep. But I never thought Eddie listened to anything I said, day or night. I stared at him. "Bad dreams. I miss her, so of course she's part of my sadness."

He shook his head. "No, it's not her you talk about."

A creepy-crawly feeling started up the back of my neck. The same feeling I got whenever I thought about that night. A feeling I shoved away as soon as it started. "We don't have time to do this now."

I started to rise, and Matthias stopped me. "What?" I let the irritation out in my voice. It was better than fear at the moment.

"We can't afford not to do this now, Rose. You might need to listen to what he has to say. He isn't the one who's been in denial for years. Maybe there's some insight you need to get you to…Rose, all of this depends on you. On how far you're willing to go."

I turned back to Eddie, who stared at me with what looked like sympathy. Again, a look I'd never seen on his face before. He gave me a sad smile.

"You talk about that night. What you felt…saw, before your granny died. I never—" He cleared his throat. "—never believed any of it was true. You thought I saw your witch stuff as a joke…maybe I did. But what you were scared of that night, it was real. Way real."

I leaned back into the corner beside the chest, feeling more than a little shaky and wishing I had a better hiding place. "I woke up that night. Or at least I thought I did. It took a minute to realize I wasn't really awake."

This time I didn't hold back the tears as I looked over at Matthias. He didn't say anything, just moved next to me and rubbed his fingers across my hand. The touch steadied me.

"I had just turned sixteen. Granny helped me set up an altar in my room, a Sweet Sixteen altar she called it. It had stuff on it that girls like, so my mom wouldn't guess what it was."

And suddenly I knew. Clear as a bell the memory hit me, shaking down the walls I'd used to protect myself all these years.

"That's where it was, where I saw it that night."

"The cup?"

I nodded. "It was sitting in the middle of the altar and…and at first I was just curious, you know. It felt so magickal. I could feel all this energy around me, pulling at me. It was all over the room, like sparks floating all around. And the cup, it was like it called to me. Called me by name. So I walked over to it, and I reached for it."

I looked down at the book in my lap, and I wanted

to toss it, to throw it across the room as hard as I could as the memories I'd held back so long flooded me. Instead I clutched it tighter, half afraid that if I let it go, I wouldn't remember, and we would all die. I cleared my throat.

"When I reached for it, when my fingers had almost touched it, the people carved on it, they started screaming. It scared me so bad I froze, like I was paralyzed. I couldn't move forward or back, I just stood there. I didn't understand what they were saying, only that they were crying and none of the sounds were happy ones. I think that's what made me realize it was a dream. As loud as they were screaming my dad would've been in my room in a heartbeat. I put my hands over my ears and started crying. Then all of a sudden they stopped. Just like that, it was quiet, and I could move again. Crazy as it sounds, it was like I needed to touch, like I had to touch it. When I did...when I did, I heard another scream. Only one voice, one scream, and it ripped my heart out."

I looked up at Matthias, and he knew. I could tell it from the look on his face.

"It was my grandmother's voice and the scream, it was like nothing I'd ever heard come out of her mouth. It was full of...full of pain. Beyond pain, agony. Like someone or something was killing her. The next thing I knew, it was morning and my dad was shaking me awake, telling me we had to go to the hospital. A neighbor had found my grandmother at the bottom of her stairs. She was dead."

"You didn't kill her, Rose."

I heard Matthias' words through the ache the memory brought with it. Given the choice, I preferred the haze of not knowing. I shook my head, wishing more that everyone and everything would go back to the way it was than believing I could actually accomplish that. That much magick was definitely beyond me. Matthias tilted my chin up and stared me in the face.

"I'm hoping the knowledge you need is in that letter."

He looked down at my lap. I'd almost forgotten the book lying there. The envelope lay half in and half out of the book.

With the tips of my fingers, as if it were a bomb that could explode any minute, I slid it out, unfolded the flap and pulled out the lined paper inside. *Would I have everything explained now?* I wondered if that would make things better or worse. It didn't take long to find out. There was only one short line written on the paper. A name, Irene Joe, and a phone number written next to it.

"What is it?"

I handed the paper to Matthias. "More what it isn't. It isn't any help."

Chapter Fourteen

"You do understand that I don't have any idea what I'm doing. Not that I don't want to, although I don't want to."

I put the phone down one more time and started to pace again. I swore I heard Matthias sigh, but it might have been my imagination. Mama gave me the same smile she gave me every time I tried to work out a new spell. In spite of its rather worn appearance, it was meant to be encouraging. I deep breathed through the panic churning in my stomach.

Mama hadn't been as much help as I'd hoped when I woke her up, thinking she might know something about the cup. All the talk about Granny Claire seemed to have bothered her. I wondered if there were things she was in denial about. Maybe we both could work on our issues when all this was over. If Vigil didn't take care of our issues for us. She told me she'd known little of my grandmother's practice. It wasn't the first time I realized Granny Claire had kept her mouth shut about a lot of what she did. And who she was.

I glanced around the table, trying to clear my head. Eddie sat beside me, drooling over the pie in the center of the table. I shoved it toward him.

"Here. Surely you still remember where the forks are, Eddie. Have at it."

"He can't." Matthias gently pushed the pie back

from Eddie. "He doesn't, um, operate in that department anymore."

My face must have looked as blank as my brain felt because Matthias continued.

"He can't eat, Rose. He isn't able to anymore."

"Oh." I felt the blush start. *Shit, I know that. What was happening to my brain?*

Matthias reached for my hand for what I hoped would turn out to be some comfort. Instead he slapped the phone back into it.

"Make the call, Rose. Get it over with."

His words hit me like a fist in the gut. What was I doing? I was stepping down that same path that killed Granny Claire. Was I crazy? I dialed Irene Joe's number.

"Hello, Rose." Her voice had that musical lilt to it that Navajos have, and it took me a minute to realize she shouldn't have known who was calling. And shouldn't have known my name. I sure as hell hadn't recognized hers when I saw it on the paper.

"Hello." My throat felt dry and scratchy. "Um, I take it this is Irene."

"Yes." She chuckled. "This is Irene. I'm assuming you finally read your grandmother's letter."

"Well, it only took me twelve years to do it. Hope you haven't been waiting all the time."

"I have, but we don't need to go into that. I can imagine you have a lot of questions."

"You could say that. What I'm really in need of is a cup my grandmother had."

"I think your questions can come first."

I glanced around the table, my gaze landing on Eddie. He was starting to look worse, if that were possible. I'd noticed his words were slowly going back to the garbled speech he'd had when Matthias first raised him. I didn't know how much longer he would be coherent, but I got the feeling it wasn't really a long time. What he would turn into after that, if I didn't get him back in the grave, wasn't something I wanted to think about. But nothing lately was what I wanted to think about so I figured it would get its turn sooner rather than later. I tried to focus on the woman on the phone.

"I'm kind of on a tight schedule here. I really need some answers right away. We can probably start with who are you and why do you know me? I mean, other than the fact that you knew my grandmother. And don't tell me you're a friend. Tonight everybody wants to claim to be my friend and help me out, but so far I'm not impressed."

She laughed. Guess I didn't impress her either.

"The cup is ready for you, but getting the answers to your questions will make you ready for it. You have the picture of it still?"

Now how did she know that? I was beginning to think I'd wasted my time with everyone else. Clearly Irene Joe knew everything I needed to know.

"I do. Tell me where you are, and I'll meet you."

"Do this first. Take the picture. Feed it three drops of your blood. Ask your questions. Then burn the picture. After you do that, call me back. I'll tell you where I am then."

She hung up before I could say anything else. My fountain of information had run dry. I glanced around the table at the eyes that stared at me before lowering my own gaze to the picture of the cup.

"If you all will excuse me, I'm going to go feed my picture."

As I started toward the door, Matthias laid a hand on my arm.

"Would you like me to ward you?"

I nodded, not sure I wanted to be alone with him, but real sure I didn't want to be alone with myself. As if she'd read my thoughts, Mama rose and joined us, then Eddie fell in line, shuffling along behind us. Guess everyone wanted to watch the show.

We walked to the greenhouse in silence. Matthias held the door open for me as he gave me what I'm sure he thought was an encouraging look. He really needed to practice.

"You can do this, Rose."

I wanted to tell him it didn't matter whether I could or not. There was no choice, no going back. Maybe I'd get answers and maybe I wouldn't. Maybe Irene was just another Vigil trying to use me. Maybe this whole night was a dream. But dream or not, until I woke up I had to keep moving forward. I looked him in the eye.

"I have to do this."

Drawing in the rich scent of the greenhouse, I sat down in the center of it, trying not to remember what Eddie had looked like lying there. From my pocket I pulled out the little knife I'd picked up on my way out of the kitchen and stared down at the picture in front of me. It was only paper and ink, I kept telling myself. Only paper and ink. Yet I heard it even as the words echoed in my head. I heard the cries, the sounds of pain and anger, of torment. Before I could run, I pricked my finger and squeezed out three drops, my gaze glued to them as they dropped onto the paper.

My focus for meditation had never been great, but now I stared hard at the wavering image of carved faces and silently asked them to take me where they were. Or at least that was the plan. I figured that was what the cup was about, the people on it. Whatever they represented or wherever they were must be the open doorway.

"Who am I?" I whispered.

My fingers were trembling when I lit the edge of the paper and dropped it into my little cauldron. I stared into the rising smoke and the more I looked, the more I felt something stir inside me, like Rip Van Winkle waking from a long sleep. I opened my heart chakra with the simple chant Granny had taught me. From inside my heart, I felt a need to speak, to accept. I wasn't sure yet what I was accepting, so I asked instead. I let myself relax into the flow of energy building around me. Once I did, I felt my body slip away, felt the lines between here and the realm beyond blur. With one more breath, I gave focus to the power gathering around me.

"Show me what you are. Show me who I am."

Chapter Fifteen

Like an idiot I'd thought there would be this nice floaty feeling when it happened. Trance states weren't something I had much experience with, but they always sounded pleasant and dreamy. I should've remembered all those sci-fi movies and novels that talked about how it hurt like hell.

One moment I could feel my body and the next I felt my soul being ripped through my skin, forced to fight its way through bone and muscle by some cosmic commander. My mouth opened to scream, but the air whooshed out of my gut instead, sending me choking into a nether realm of dark skies and stormy rumblings. I could've sworn lightning flashed on both sides and a strange gurgling sound roared up around me. It could've been the sound of me trying to breathe.

After a moment I hit solid ground really hard. Dust flew up into my eyes, my nose, and my mouth. I rolled onto my side, trying to suck enough air into my lungs to stop them from screaming. That's when I noticed the feet. Bare feet. Lean, strong and sturdy looking bare feet. *What is it with feet showing up to scare the shit out of me?* I closed my eyes.

"Are you quite finished?"

The voice was male, cultured and loaded with disgust.

"I can't breathe," I croaked, the words scraping

across my throat with a knifing pain. The feet didn't move. I rolled my gaze up to the dark black eyes attached to them.

He looked down at me as if I was an idiot. "Of course you can't breathe. We're under a thousand tons or more of rock. There is no air to breathe."

"I need air." I got the words out between gasps.

He shook his head. "No, you don't."

"What?" I shook my head, wondering why all my dreams were now nightmares.

His sigh echoed in the empty space around us. "You. Don't. Need. To. Breathe. Here."

"Uh, hello." I flopped onto my back, vaguely aware of my resemblance to a beached whale trying to turn over. "I'd like to stay alive."

"That's exactly the point." He reached down and gripped my hand, pulling me to my feet with a jerk. I started to scream but gulped for the air around me instead. He rolled his eyes.

"Do you know nothing?"

From the look on his face, I could tell what he thought the answer to that question was. I started to tell him I knew more about greeting company than he did, but I was still trying to breathe so I left that comment for later.

"Did you really think I brought your physical body through the veil?" He shook his head. "We have so much work to do. First lesson, your body is breathing. That's what's keeping it alive while it waits for you. So you can stop with the silly sucking sounds. You don't need to breathe here. It's actually a plus."

I felt like telling him nothing I'd experienced here so far could be called a plus, including him, but the moment I opened my mouth, he turned away. Sort of like he didn't want to hear anything else I had to say. Maybe I'd be doing him a favor by cluing him in on what hospitality entailed, a detail I'd be more than happy to share just as soon as I stopped dying.

Deciding it was either trust him or go insane, I stopped trying to catch the breath that had obviously remained back in the real world. The moment I did, my body, or whatever this facsimile of it was, calmed down. Without the adrenaline surge of my survival instincts, I had a chance to really get a look at my surroundings.

It was a sandstone cavern, and looked like what I thought that place where they took the President and other VIPs in case of nuclear attack would look like. Modern track lighting beamed down over a desk with computers and equipment that couldn't possibly be under tons of rock. One wall was covered with maps of all kinds. Beneath it stood a metal shelf holding more maps, some old but others clearly new. A long table in the center held more maps and folders with papers spilled out of them. The whole place looked like Command Central for the next world war.

My mind, which had been having a tough enough time lately, simply refused to process any more anachronisms. The idea of an underground bunker with no air and all the trappings of a military installation sent it into system overload. Nothing was real any longer as far as my poor brain was concerned. It didn't trust my eyes or any other part of me. This place, whatever the hell it was, was one step too much for my sense of logic. I shook my head.

"Where in the hell am I?"

"Right at the gates of it."

It took a minute for that answer to penetrate. "What?"

He made the disgusted face again. "There's obviously been a severe lack of success in your mentoring so far. I suppose I'll get the blame for that, too." His gaze rolled up and down me. "I've tried to tell them it happens with some generations. But I'm expected to work miracles with what little I'm given, so here we are. Late bloomers are the worst."

The look on his face told me I had a long way to go before I measured up to his expectations. I suddenly felt like an extra in *GI Jane*, the one that didn't survive boot camp. Since I needed a moment to adjust my spinning equilibrium to the long strange trip I was apparently on, I let my gaze wander over my captor before I answered his slur.

He stood maybe five ten in bare feet. Dressed in a loose cotton tunic and pants with a wide black belt, he looked a bit like a shortened version of Bruce Lee. Not that he was anywhere near as attractive as Bruce. From his military-style buzz cut to the wide-leg stance with hands on his hips, he was the epitome of every reason I had avoided studying any kind of martial arts. Guys who can twist their bodies in pretzel shapes so they can break all the bones in your arms didn't sound like the kind of mentor I was looking for. They were right up there with yoga instructors and the size 0 models who got their kicks teaching Zumba classes. I met his look of disgust with one of my own.

"Maybe there would've been more success if I'd known anything about…" I waved my hand around me, "this."

"This," he sneered as he made an exaggerated imitation of my movements, "is all you really needed to know. It should have been the most important thing you learned in your whole life. This is what you were made for, the only reason for your puny little existence."

"I was made to live in hell?" *Boy, didn't that put a damper on my search for future happiness.*

He folded his arms across his chest. "Why not? You've kept me there for twelve years."

"What?" I knew it was repetitive, but my poor mind couldn't come up with anything better. This was so not what I'd expected.

"Where's the cup?" I decided to start with the most important point and work my way away from my obvious shortcomings. The less Bruce Lite knew about those the better, as far as I was concerned.

"The cup?"

He moved so fast I didn't even get time to blink. One minute he was walking away from me and the next he'd invaded my personal space. He raised a hand, and I had a nanosecond to think before he grabbed the front of my shirt and lifted me off the ground.

"You have the cup, do you not?"

I wriggled myself loose from his grasp, although it was more likely that he just let go. "No. I've only got a drawing of it."

"You didn't drink from the cup?"

"No."

"No? What do you mean no? What in the world are you waiting for? It's a point in your favor that Michael Himself decreed the cup be left here for you. Although from what I've seen so far, I cannot imagine what could have inspired him to believe you would be worthy of it."

"Michael?"

"Do you know nothing?"

"I know I'm getting tired of participating in conversations I don't understand. I know you're kind of an asshole, and I came here for help, not ridicule. I know—"

"Enough. I may as well have been sent a baby for all the knowledge you possess. Can I at least assume you know where the cup is?"

"Maybe."

He narrowed his eyes at me. "Why are you here?"

"I'm here to find out who I am. What I am. That was the spell I performed to get me here."

He snorted. "Your *spell* has little to do with your arrival in this place. Had Michael not wished it, you could never have crossed into this realm."

"Okay, so where is this Michael, and how do I talk to him?" I wanted to add instead of wasting my time with you, but I was supposed to be the one with the good manners.

"This Michael, as you put it, is the Archangel Michael, and you don't talk to him."

"What? But…everyone has been talking about my destiny, my lineage. What does an archangel have to do with that? I worship the Goddess. I don't know anything about angels. I mean, I know some Wiccans are into that, but I've never…" I looked around me. "Wait a minute, I'm not dead, am I? And who are you?"

"You may call me Jokyu, and no, you're not dead. Although given how little you seem to know, I find that fact miraculous. I am your trainer. Not that I've had any chance to train you nor will I until you stop fooling around and drink from the cup. As if you haven't wasted enough of my time already."

He waved a hand toward an entire gym set-up I hadn't noticed in one corner of the room. It would have been really impressive if it hadn't been scaled down to a size for a child.

"This was meant for me?" I stared at the miniature equipment with doubt.

"You were meant to arrive as a child."

"And when I didn't, you couldn't change it? What kind of preparation is that?"

"The kind that was prepared for you not to show up at all."

Thanks for the support, I thought. "You know, maybe if someone had come and talked to me about all this, even after my grandmother died, then I would have been more prepared."

"And maybe," he sneered, "if you were in any way connected to the power that lies in the palm of your hands, you wouldn't have wandered around for years, letting everyone else tend to your duties."

He moved like lightning again and grabbed me by the arm before I could pull away. Before I could yell at him to let go, he dragged me to an old chart hanging from the wall. Most of it looked ancient and tattered, but the ink at the bottom looked a bit fresher than the rest. At the top of the chart, in those fancy calligraphy letters I always admired, was written "The Lineage of Michael, Guardian of the Watchtower of the South". Jokyu thumped his hand against the chart.

"As for Michael, he is your destiny, and your lineage. He is your liege and the one for whom your life is given. He is your life. At least the most important part of it."

"He's part of it?"

"You are a descendant of Michael's. That is what qualifies you to drink from the cup in the first place." He gave me another one of those looks. "There is certainly nothing else I see about you that would make you worthy of becoming a ShadowWalker, were it not for Michael's blood in your veins."

Maybe it was the effect of a very long night, but my head started to spin as I felt the need to breathe again. It wasn't enough that I had dug up my dead husband, had some guy I'd just met raise him as a zombie, spent an hour chitchatting with the guy who killed him, and then found myself shoved through tons of rock into the heart of a mountain where there was no air. I reached out a hand to grab onto something, someone, even if it was my newfound tormentor. But my hand passed right through him, and that was the last of my stamina. Everything around me turned black as I hit the floor.

When I opened my eyes again, Jokyu stood over me frowning, hands on hips.

"If you're going to do that every time you learn something, it's going to be very difficult to train you. And you're far enough behind in your training as it is."

Learn something? He said it like he'd told me tomorrow was going to be rainy. Then it hit me.

"Wait a minute. Spirits can't faint."

I shot him an accusing glare as he hauled me up by one hand. He gave a disgusted snort.

"Exactly. You probably scared your friends to death when you fainted, if they even recovered from the whole gasping like an out of water fish thing earlier."

"You mean I fainted in both places? And why is it you can touch me but I can't touch you?"

He just stared at me, his lip curled in an obvious sneer. We were so not going to get along.

I dragged my fragile mind back to the next question on my list. "You can't be serious with this whole angel Michael stuff. The Archangels are…they're…well, they're celestial beings. Heavenly beings. I mean, Guardians of the Watchtowers and all. Hello." I waved my hand in front of him. "Puny human here."

"You don't have to convince me."

"Me? A descendant of the archangel Michael?" I'd had so many twists and turns this night that I wasn't sure this one could register with my mind. I glanced up at the chart. "Just how many descendants does he have?"

He shrugged, and I felt my eye twitch. I was coming to understand that whenever a male shrugged it meant I probably wasn't going to like what came out of their mouth next.

"Angels live a long time. They get to know a lot of people, a lot of them female. Michael is quite handsome."

"Angelically speaking?" I couldn't keep the sarcasm out of my voice, in spite of the fact it didn't seem like the smartest idea to piss off a celestial being. Maybe Michael was off doing something else and wouldn't know I'd been snarky about his love life. Then I thought of something. "Wait a minute. I thought angels were, you know, asexual. Like sterile or something."

"And you say you are a follower of the Goddess." He shook his head and sighed. "How could one who has felt Her presence believe she would deny the gift of sexuality to any who belonged to Her? Your very existence should tell you that myth holds no truth. It stems only from the fears of petty men."

"My existence has been pretty ordinary up till now. It would almost deny the truth of that. Believe me, nobody at any of the family reunions stood out as particularly angelic."

"Genetics isn't always pleasant."

"Are you insinuating I'm the off branch of the family tree?"

"I'm telling you that you've wasted enough time already. You don't really have more to throw away on debating stupid myths."

"Okay. We'll lay that one aside for now. But I do have some questions that I need answered."

"The only question you need to answer is, are you willing to drink from the cup, to take up your role as Michael's ShadowWalker?"

"ShadowWalker? What's a ShadowWalker? What am I supposed to do? How can I answer that when I don't know anything about it?"

His sigh echoed off the stone walls. Without another word, he turned and walked toward a rough stone table in the far corner of the room. It had the feel of age and the closer I got, the more power I felt. A chest of what looked like pure gold sat on top of it. It was shiny but plain, just a golden square. Lifting the lid from the chest, Jokyu pulled out what looked like a scroll. With more reverence than he'd given anything else, he turned back to me and motioned me over to him.

"In here you will find some of your answers. The rest you will have to find on your own." He gave me a speculative look. "You might start by asking your companions."

I stared at him. "My companions?"

"I am not the only one who has been forced to wait on you. You might consider that when you return to your friends."

He held up a hand when I opened my mouth.

"Read this. Then we shall talk again."

I took the scroll from his hand and just stared at it. It felt more like cloth than paper, which told me something about its age as well. I breathed in the scent of it, sandalwood and spice, letting its ancient feel brush along my skin, delicate yet powerful. And there was power here, in every fiber of paper, every drop of ink. It flowed out over me with the first taste of reassurance I'd gotten since Leon woke me stumbling in. As I held the scroll in my hands, I found myself asking the question I always did when I sought answers to my problems. *Do I trust the Goddess and believe in Her love for me?* It was a simple question, but I always found the answer reassuring. She spoke to my heart each time I asked it, and this time was no different. She didn't ever give me flowers and airy feelings, but She always let me know of Her presence. I knew beyond doubt She stood here in this mountain with me. Her voice was clear and strong in my head. With it echoing through my heart, I opened the scroll.

I knew if I opened it there might be some of the answers I needed. Just like I knew if I opened it, if I read the words written on its pages, I could never go back to the way things were. The magick the paper held made that truth clear. From this moment on, I would know. No matter what I did with that knowledge, I would know what I'd been avoiding since the day my grandmother died. I could never go back to innocence or denial.

"What will I be after I read this?" I murmured.

I felt her then. Granny Claire stood across from me when I looked up. She was in kick-ass mode again, the power I'd always been so impressed by radiating off her. The look on her face was serious and solemn.

You'll be who you are, Rose.

I shook my head. "I'm not ready for this."

Ready or not, here it comes.

Through the tears in my eyes, I watched her fade away. Don't leave me, I thought. Her answer echoed in the stone around me. *I never do.*

I untied the leather strip that bound it and smoothed the scroll down with both hands. In spite of my fears, the tingle of its energy was warm and, in a strange way, loving. The ink was clear and bright, as if it had been written today. But the magick told me it had been written longer ago than I could imagine. It told a story, of a great battle, an uprising of pain and loss and evil. It told of both human and other realms, of hate and of love, of balance and of power. And it told of a spring.

I knew from my own studies that places of water such as springs and lakes were portals for magick. I had never connected that idea to good magick or bad. To me all magick was good. But this spring, this place that the story told me was the domain of the ShadowWalker, was made of more than water. It was the gathering of shadows, of pain and sorrow, of secrets and hidden motives that took desire to an evil end. And all that negative energy had created a doorway that opened to those who desired to bring evil into the world. Those who desired to create more shadows to hide who and what they were, and the things that they did in the waters there.

It wasn't the only one. There was a portal in each of the four directions, each one guarded by a descendant of the Guardian of the Watchtower of that direction. A descendant of angels. It felt eerie to read my own name on the ancient paper. Eerie and not altogether pleasant. It was even spelled right. According to the scroll, Michael was the Guardian of the South, and I was the next in line to serve him as a ShadowWalker, a sort of supernatural bounty hunter who kept tabs on things that came through the portal that shouldn't. And made sure they went back through the portal. Law enforcement had never been a dream of mine. Sometimes family legacies don't really seem to fit the genetic make-up of the individual. If Michael's bounty hunting blood flowed through mine, it had been quite recessive for the last twenty-eight years.

I glanced over at the miniature gym set-up and sighed. Did my celestial ancestor know that I didn't even have a gym membership these days? The closest thing I had to exercise equipment was a Pilates DVD that was still in the package. Archangel blood or not, I was so screwed.

The story ended with a charge, a sort of call to arms for those willing to take up the cup and drink from the pool of shadows. Those who were willing to become a ShadowWalker. I closed the scroll and wrapped the leather strip back around it. My fingers trembled as I placed it back into the chest. Jokyu was standing behind me when I turned. I took a deep breath, hoping he had nothing more to tell me that would end with me on the floor again.

"Okay, I've read the story. And it kind of explains things, but I have to tell you none of this seems real to me. At least not in a way I can wrap my head around right now. I have some more pressing problems than guarding a spring. If I don't get them solved, I won't be around to guard anything. Right now what is real to me is the fact that I will be going to jail for murder if I don't get my dead ex-husband back in the ground. There's another man who claims he's the one who owns this cup, and he's willing to kill me to get it. Then there's my grandmother. Why didn't she tell me any of this?"

He sighed deep enough for the whole underworld to hear. "Perhaps she knew you were not up to the task."

Something inside me snapped. Maybe everybody else might have thought that, but my grandmother loved me. And she believed in me. I'd had enough, done enough, seen enough in the last fourteen hours to know I didn't intend to put up with many more attacks on my character or changes to my world. I moved right up into his face and poked him in the chest. The surprise wiped boredom right out of his expression.

"Look, you sanctimonious jackass, I'm not here to play your stupid games or let you abuse me for your own amusement." I took another step toward him, and he almost stepped back. The momentum gave my anger more fuel. "I've got questions. You've got answers, and you're going to share them. No ifs, ands, or buts. I'm sorry I don't bring you great honor. It's too bad you can't brag about me in the trainers' lounge with your buddies. Sorry you got stuck with such a pitiful excuse for a student, but stuck you are and neither of us is going to get unstuck until you get down off your high horse and start giving me some information. Real, useful information, not hyped up garbage masquerading as riddles."

He took a step back this time, but the look on his face was more like he'd smelled something disgusting. "Oh, I see. You just come in here and demand to know whatever you need to know so you can waltz out and do your job without having to put any effort, any *skill*"—he leaned into my face as he stressed it—"into doing your job. I do the work, and you're the great and powerful ShadowWalker, is that it?"

A large part of me wanted to say yes, that was exactly it and he needed to start doing that asap. Instead I took a breath and searched for some control.

"I'm not asking you to do everything. Just to give me some of the information I need to do it myself. I need you to answer my questions."

"What questions?"

I swallowed hard, wondering if there was room in my throat to get the words past the lump there. "How did my grandmother die? Was she doing something wrong and that's what killed her? Did the cup kill her? I mean, all my life I've had this image, this idea of this wonderful woman who saw only light, who gave only good, who kept the Rede. Now I've got to know the truth about her. I've got to know who she was, and what really happened to her."

I never saw him move. One minute he stood there

sneering at me, and the next I was flat on my back with him standing over me. It seemed to be the only position he wanted me to assume around him. There wasn't only a sneer on his face now, there was outright loathing. He bent down to me, almost flinching as if getting near me was a odious task.

"The only thing you need to know, you stupid girl, is who you are. Who you really are. When you find that out, come back to me. Maybe I'll answer your questions."

His hands reached out to me, and the next thing I knew I was flat on my back on my greenhouse floor.

Chapter Sixteen

"You knew about all this. All along you knew."

I glared at Matthias. We'd come back to the kitchen after my somewhat frightening return. I'd opened my eyes to a ring of concerned faces, but the one I'd zeroed in on was his. Jokyu's words kept echoing in my head. I'd been set up, and by more people than just Vigil.

"Not all of it."

The hedging in his voice made me angrier. His face showed nothing. I was getting damned tired of wondering what was going on behind that unreadable expression. For a minute, I thought he wasn't going to say anything, which only made me madder. I wasn't going to be ignored anymore, no matter what I had to do to get that point across. Maybe he felt the anger; maybe he was just ready to talk. Either way, he finally spoke.

"What I can tell you is the night your grandmother died, it wasn't because you picked up the cup. That much you can know for sure. As for the rest…there are other things that are far more relevant right now you need to focus on. I think the rest of the conversation can wait till another time."

"Uh-uh. No more stalling. And don't use that tone with me ever again. I don't need you or anyone else telling me what to do."

He arched a brow, and it took all I had not to slap

him.

"I'm about done listening to what everyone else thinks. I've heard a whole lot of opinions the last few hours, opinions of me, of my skill and of what I should be doing. What I haven't heard is any answers to the questions that are important to me. So you either give me the answers I need, or I take Eddie and go to the police, and whatever happens, happens. This is your last chance. Exactly what do you know that you haven't told me? And how do you know it?"

"You aren't going to drop this, are you?"

I shook my head. "You keep telling me you didn't come out tonight on a whim. What was it that brought you here? What do you know about me that interests you? What do you get out of this?"

"I really am on your side, Rose." He tried to use both the eyes and the voice on me. I knew how much the night had worn on me by the fact that neither of them had any effect. "You can trust that."

"I'm not sure there's anything about tonight I can trust, beside the fact I don't know shit about a lot of things."

"Trust this, Rose. There are a lot of people who want to help. There's a lot I can't tell you, because I don't know."

"Tell me what you do know. You want me to trust you, then talk to me. Right here, right now."

He sat down, pulling me down into the chair beside him. "I don't know all the answers, Rose. I'm not supposed to tell you anything. That's the rule. You have to come to this decision yourself."

"How can I come to any decision when I don't know any of the information to base it on? How is that fair? And whose rules are we talking about? Who is it that's deciding things about my life?"

"It isn't fair. You should know a lot of things that you don't. And it isn't fair to ask you to make any decision without all the information, but that's the way it is, and I can't change that."

"I don't give a shit about your rules. Or anybody else's rules." Even an archangel's, I thought. "You knew what was going on, and you didn't tell me. Is that why you came to my house in the middle of the night? Why you raised Eddie? Why you've been following me around, letting me stumble around in the dark without saying a word about any of this? You knew the answers all along, and you let me keep asking the questions. You let me go through…"

I couldn't finish it. I couldn't think about all that had happened to me in the last fourteen hours, all that had changed. My whole life had exploded right in front of me, and the man I thought was my knight in shining armor had known all along it would. Had watched me watch the explosion happen without a word of caution.

"Knights don't do that."

"Excuse me?"

"No, I don't excuse you." I poked Matthias in the chest. He didn't move. "I don't understand you. And I'm pretty sure I shouldn't trust you. Not anymore."

He reached for my hand, and I jerked it back.

"Rose, after all that's happened I think it would be pretty foolish not to trust me. I'm here, and I'm here for you."

"Who were you here for an hour ago? Who were you watching out for when you let me stumble through this mess without saying a word?"

"I couldn't tell you about the cup."

"Couldn't or wouldn't? What was it, some kind of test you wanted to see if I could pass? Did you and Alexis decide on this as some kind of initiation?"

"No. I had to follow the rules. Only your grandmother could have told you the answers to your questions. She's the only one who really knew the answers. The rest of us—"

"The rest of you? Exactly how many people have been keeping this little secret?"

"Everyone who takes on the role of a ShadowWalker makes their own choice. You had to make your own choice. And to be truthful, we don't know all the answers. Most of us only know the basics. We couldn't step in before and now…well, we felt like we had to give you room to remember what happened with your grandmother. That was the only way you could make the choice yourself."

I sank down in the chair. "The grandmother who told me nothing about what she was, what I am. Or what I was supposed to be. Why?"

He shook his head. "I don't know that answer. Maybe your parents wouldn't allow her to train you. Maybe she thought she had time."

"I was sixteen. When was she going to get around to it?"

"I don't know that either, Rose. All I know is that the cup comes with certain conditions, the main one being the requirement that each ShadowWalker choose their path."

"If it be thy will, let this cup pass from me."

I don't know where the quote came from, some latent Sunday school lesson probably. Matthias stared at me, more sympathy in his eyes than I had seen there all night.

"The cup came to you that night because it already knew your grandmother was going to die. It was doing what the magick designed it to do. When one cupbearer passes, the cup comes to the next in line. Since your mother had no magick, it moved to the next person. That would have been you."

"Would have been?"

"If you had drunk from the cup that night, the line of succession would be filled. Your grandmother would have passed the duty to you, and everything would have been as it should have. You would have been trained for your…destiny a long time ago."

"But I fucked things up."

"You were young and untrained, Rose, and you had no knowledge of what was going on. That wasn't your fault. Your grandmother probably planned to tell you when you were an adult, but never got the chance. She didn't see her own death coming in time."

"None of that tells me why you were willing to come out tonight, to raise Eddie, to follow me to Vigil's. None of that tells me what you get out of all this. Why are you here, Matthias?"

"It's my job to be here."

"Your job."

He nodded. "The elders—"

"Elders? What elders?"

"The elders of the magickal community in this area. Alexis is one of them."

"So that explains her interest in me."

He nodded. "They are the reservoirs of knowledge, that the rest of us can go to when we need to know something. If they're willing to tell it."

"From the look on your face they aren't always helpful."

He snorted. "Have you always found Alexis helpful when you wanted to know something?"

Not hardly, I thought. The woman was a riddle wrapped up in an enigma and laid out like a puzzle. "No, I can't say she is."

"Well the rest are just like her."

"And they sent you to me?"

"They...made me aware of you, but not because they thought things would turn out like they have. I'm sure they had no idea you would find Eddie or need to call me. What they did fear was that, as time continued to pass and you didn't uncover your legacy, one day Vigil would make a move on you. They weren't sure how that would end."

"So they decided to just wait and see."

He nodded.

"Because there are rules, and they can't break them?"

He nodded again.

I stood up and began to pace. "And now? What's their great and useful plan now that things have gotten all fucked up?"

"It's not so much their plan that's important. The ball's pretty much in your court."

"Or the cup, you mean."

"The cup, yes. Now you have a choice to make. It's clear the cup has stayed to wait for you to make that choice. It could've moved on, but for some reason it didn't. I have to believe that reason has something to do with you, with what you bring to the table."

"And if my answer is no? What happens then? Tell me about Vigil. What happens if he gets the cup? Can he take the cup from me and use it, in a magickal sense? Can he drink from the cup and use its power?"

"According to the elders, he's not a descendant of Michael, so no, he can't drink from the cup. But there is a way for him to control it."

"A way?"

He gave me a cautious look.

I wanted to tell him that if I thought there was anywhere to run and hide I would've already done it, but I figured he knew that. I also figured I did not want to hear what he was going to say next, but he was probably going to say it anyway. We were both turning out to be pretty predictable.

"If you're dead and he has possession of the cup, the next descendant in line can't drink from it. It's not so much that he gains the power of the cup as he can block the power of it."

"How?"

"I really don't know enough to understand exactly what would happen. I just know it would be bad. Vigil has been…moving a lot of energy for the last few years, for lack of a better explanation. He's been behind a lot of things that have brought a lot of bad magick to this area. I don't know exactly why or where he's getting it from. According to the elders, he didn't have that kind of power before your grandmother died. They're scared now."

"About me?"

"More about Vigil. About the power he seems to have found."

"They know where it comes from?"

"I think they know some things. Not everything."

"And what did they tell you? What is his connection to the cup? To my grandmother?"

"They believe his family has, or had, some connection to the line of Michael."

"What connection? If he isn't a descendant of Michael then what connection could he have?"

"I don't know. I don't know if they know. The magick surrounding the cup is very old and very well guarded. And what your grandmother knew she took to her grave."

"Too bad she didn't take the cup there, too." I shook my head as I sat back down beside him. "But their fear is that he could hold onto the cup and keep anyone else from using its magick. That would pretty much give the bad things free rein."

"If he could have done that I think he would have done it years ago."

"Except he didn't have the cup."

"So he says."

"And you don't believe him?"

"I think he knows more about where the cup is than he's told you. I think he needs you to remove it from wherever it is. Taking it from you after that would be pretty simple."

"Thanks for the vote of support."

He shrugged. "It's not meant as a slap at you. You didn't know anything about any of this. I think he believed he could get you to give him the cup, and you would never know anything about it."

"Then Eddie did something stupid and got himself killed."

"Eddie messed up his simple plan, so he went to

the more complicated one."

"The one where I get killed so he can keep the cup."

He nodded.

"Seems like a lot of people have kept back information from me." I sighed. "If I say yes to this destiny, does the cup go away where he can't touch it?"

He looked away. "There is a problem with that."

"Why does that not surprise me? So what's the problem?"

"In the normal course of things, the departing ShadowWalker takes the cup back with them beyond the grave after the new one drinks from it and accepts the job. The cup then won't reappear until the current ShadowWalker dies."

"But Granny's gone. And the cup is still here."

He nodded again, frowning this time. "Yes."

"Can she come and get it now?"

"Your grandmother? A spirit, a ghost, no longer possesses a corporeal body. To carry the cup would take the ability to, well, carry it. I don't think that's something your grandmother can do anymore."

"But we have to get rid of the cup. Otherwise Vigil can still kill me and gain the cup. Will it leave on its own after I drink?"

He shrugged, avoiding my eyes. "Possibly."

"I was wrong."

"About what?"

"You aren't full of information. You're full of maybes."

Matthias stood and offered me his hand. "Then maybe we can find the answers you need by following your grandmother's clue."

"Maybe." *And maybe that's just another hole for me to fall into.* But I kept that thought to myself.

Chapter Seventeen

The wood and tarpaper hogan stood like a sentinel doing duty alone in the desert. All five feet of her stood in the doorway as if she'd been waiting for us to arrive since I hung up the phone. As I got out of the car, I took in the details of the woman I hoped could explain who I was.

Irene Joe was small but not delicate, at least not in the sense of fragile. Her hair crowned her head like a silver wreath, framing a face of richest bronze. Each feature etched on it held an exotic beauty that whispered *there's more within*. I'd expected traditional dress, but she wore loose black pants and a soft red velvet top on which lay a beautiful turquoise and silver necklace. This night hadn't brought me anything else I'd expected so things were right on course. Her feet were bare in spite of the night chill and her voice held a guttural timbre that let the hearer know upfront there would be no beating around the bush.

"So you finally found it, huh?"

I didn't know whether she meant her home or everything else I'd found recently, but there was no mistaking the impatience behind the words. The closer I got, the more the weird feeling of *déjà vu* crept over me. She looked a thousand years old, not in physical deterioration but in the power that vibrated around her. Like I'd come to the mountain and there stood the one

167

who knew it all.

"I know you."

The words were out of my mouth before I could stop them, but she only smiled as she waved us inside. Bigger than I'd expected and cozy in a way that didn't match the woman standing beside me, the space beckoned those who entered to sit, to rest. But this wasn't the night for such things so I stood like an awkward child instead.

"Your granny and I had a few talks. She brought you to see me once, when you were still pretty little."

I shook my head to try and clear it. There had been so much to absorb the last few hours, it was a wonder I didn't hear sloshing from my brain melting down within my head.

"No, it's more than that. I know you. Like, I've seen you and not when I was a child. Or not only then. I've seen you…"

"In your dreams?"

She was still smiling when she finished the thought I'd try to bury deep inside me, yet another revelation. I knew if I let it all out, I'd never be able to back away. I nodded.

"I've tried to contact you since your Granny died."

"In my dreams?"

She shrugged. "It was the easiest way."

I would never have pegged dreamwalking as all that easy, but that's me. "You said you tried to contact me. About the cup?"

"About a lot of things."

She sat in the old rocker that looked like the coziest piece in the room. It didn't seem to bother her to look up at me, but it made me feel even more awkward. I sat across from her on the embroidered stool. Matthias stayed by the doorway where he could keep an eye on Eddie. Over the last hour, Eddie had seemed to deteriorate a bit more. One more thing to worry about. I turned my attention back to the woman I hoped held answers instead of more questions.

"Can you be a bit more specific?" My only excuse for not even trying to keep the sarcasm out of my voice was I was nearly as tired as Eddie looked.

"Things you needed to know. Things we needed you to know. Things your grandmother didn't get the time to tell you."

"We? Is there anyone in the world besides me who doesn't know all there is to know about who I am? What I am."

"We'll get to that in a bit."

"You know I really need to get some answers from someone. If you can't do it then point me in the right direction, and I'll get out of your hair." I didn't bother to keep the irritation from my tone either. "I'm running out of time here."

My bitchiness didn't appear to faze her any more than my sarcasm had.

"You've been on borrowed time for a while now."

"That's what I keep hearing. And still nobody wants to tell me the truth, to tell me what's going on, why I have a cup waiting for me that somebody would kill to have."

Irene nodded. "You're right. The cup is a choice. That's why we're all in this mess now. To drink or not to drink is a choice those who come from the lineage of Michael must make. From your lineage, Rose, therefore you have a choice to make."

"I read it. The scroll."

I watched her face as I said it, but her expression never changed. If she was surprised, it didn't show. She tilted her head and stared at me out of her beautiful dark eyes. In spite of her thick gray hair, her face was smooth and her eyes clear and full of wonder and ancient knowledge. I don't know how I knew, but I knew my answer lay somewhere behind that steady gaze.

"Is all this true? Is this, what was in the scroll, is it what my grandmother was? Who she was?"

"Your grandmother was many things."

"Why does everybody just want to answer me with riddles? I hate riddles. Can't you just give me the simple answer?" I stood up and began to pace.

"The simple answer to who you are is yes."

I stopped and stared at her. "Yes? Yes? What does that mean?"

"You read the scroll. It's simple. Or it will be once you make your decision."

"Whether or not to drink from the cup? Jokyu didn't make it sound like things would be simple if I decided not to drink."

"I didn't say the consequences wouldn't be catastrophic. I said things would be simple. Either we have a protector or it all goes to hell in a hand basket and the world ends. Pretty simple."

I needed to get all the plain speaking people out of my life or my nerves were going to be shot.

"Okay, I get that it's all been up to me. Apparently, I've been derelict in a duty I didn't know I had."

"Drinking from the cup is up to you. Putting yourself in the position that your lineage assigns to you is up to you. You're not alone though. The rest of us are here to help. As a matter of fact, we've been holding the line while you've been, derelict, as you put it."

"Holding the line? Then why do you need me as the protector?"

"If you were looking with your Sight, you wouldn't be asking that question."

"Sight?"

"You have psychic senses already, Rose. They are why and how I was able to visit you in your dreams. And your mind is very strong. Had it been more…flexible, you would have remembered our times together. Strength can be both a help and a hindrance."

"So I need to open my psychic abilities to see what's going on around me."

"They will help you see some things you need to see. But making your choice will help more. The cup will enhance what you already have, enabling you to see into the realms beyond our own."

"So I get at least some superpowers?"

"You get a few, yes."

"I don't understand. This is all so crazy. Archangels? Michael? And why me, why my family? We haven't been part of this land forever. What about the spirits of this land? I'm not native. My family are relative newcomers to this place."

"Intermarriage is an interesting thing."

"Almost as interesting as angelic sex?" I couldn't keep the sarcasm from my voice. I probably should have been worried about offending my celestial relative. Maybe He'd decide to kill me off Himself and save Vigil the trouble.

Irene laughed, the musical sound of it rolling out of

her to fill the room. "I should think that would be far more interesting. Or at least I should hope so. As for your question, you white people killed a lot of us off."

She said it with another of the shrugs I was really getting tired of seeing from people. "And made a lot of babies with some of the ones of us who were left. Intermarriage changed the face of this land as much as anything else. Then, when you couldn't kill us outright anymore, you tried to drown us in alcohol. While we were sleeping it off you gave us gangs, TV, cell phones and modern living. Talk about your demonic assault to get rid of us. Seems only fair that a few of you get stuck with safeguarding what's left of our world."

I couldn't argue with that.

"Do you have the cup?" I let the blunt words fill the room.

"Yes."

She didn't seem bothered in the least by my question or the way it was asked. She also didn't seem interested in elaborating on her answer. We sat there staring at each other for a long moment. Something told me the ball was in my court, but there was one more thing I needed to know before I went any further.

"I need to know who Vigil is, who he was to my grandmother."

"The man who killed her."

I shook my head. "My grandmother died in a fall down the stairs."

"Your grandmother never fell anywhere. She was the most graceful person I ever knew. Jokyu saw to that."

"He trained her?"

The picture of Granny Claire with the sarcastic

trainer almost made me giggle. I'd known my grandmother was tough. She didn't have a girly bone in her body, my mother used to say. My dad just said she could take him in arm-wrestling, a feat that put her in a class by herself. He always said it with admiration.

She cackled, a surprising sound coming out of such an elegant mouth. "Older than he looks, isn't he?"

"Yes."

"Better than he seems at what he does, too. If you can get past the desire to punch him in the nuts, you'll find he can teach you what you need to know."

I wasn't sure I could get past that desire.

"But that's a problem for after your choice."

"Did my grandmother love him?"

"Your grandmother trusted him. And he betrayed that trust."

"What did she trust him to do?"

Trust was an angle I hadn't thought of before, but suddenly it occurred to me that perhaps Vigil had played a different role in my grandmother's life as a ShadowWalker than he had intimated. In spite of Matthias' warnings, I'd let myself get so wrapped up in the thought that my grandmother was romantically involved with a killer that I hadn't stopped to consider all the other possibilities. And if Granny Claire had trusted him, Vigil must have made her believe he was an ally. Vigil must also have had some powerful magick to keep her from realizing that he wasn't until it was too late.

Irene rose from the chair and walked to a small cabinet made of wood. The doors were intricately carved with lightning bolts surrounding images of the Holy People. From the top drawer inside the cabinet, she pulled out a small dreamcatcher and handed it to me.

"I assume you know what this is."

I held it, thinking she meant there was some magick to it. When I felt nothing I frowned up at her.

"What does a dreamcatcher have to do with Vigil?"

She turned and sat back down in the rocker. "Since you read the scroll, you know the story of the ShadowWalkers."

I nodded, hoping there was more to what she would say.

"ShadowWalkers fulfill the need to close the portals, to cut off the entry into our world of those beings who desire what is less than good. And they hunt those beings and ensure they are sent back through the portal."

Less than good. That was an interesting way to put it, I thought. I stared at her and she continued.

"What they do is an important thing, but the damage from having the open portal still must be repaired."

"You mean I've got to learn how to go around and fix everything the bad guys have torn apart? Just closing the portal doesn't do that?" This job was starting to look like a bit more than saving the world. If I had to go around fixing all the damage after I saved it, I knew we were screwed.

"No." She laughed. "You don't have to go door to door asking what folks' troubles are and how you can fix them. Do you understand how a dreamcatcher is supposed to work?"

"It catches the bad dreams that come to haunt you."

"The weaver weaves the dreamcatcher as a sort of

protective device, to keep out the things that would harm us. But you can also think of it as a filter for the space it's placed in. Those things that are harmful will be caught in its weaving and kept from doing any further harm until their power is dissipated."

"Okay, so I need to learn to make magickal dreamcatchers?"

"You don't. Your weaver will do that."

"My weaver?"

"Yes. Armando Vigil was your grandmother's weaver. His gift was to weave protection over the community, and your grandmother's job was to keep the portal closed. Weavers and ShadowWalkers work in tandem with each other to protect the community from those negative influences and beings that seek to bring evil to our world."

"Vigil was supposed to protect people? Something tells me he didn't get the memo on that job description."

"No, I don't think he did."

"So now he's what, weaving bad magick so he can control things? How do I fix that?"

"You cannot fix all the damage he has done. But you can stop what he's doing. Remember that something woven can be unwoven. Pull the right thread, and it all comes undone." Irene sighed. "Your grandmother had great trust in Armando. Too much trust, as it turned out. It happens sometimes. The temptation of the kind of magick, the kind of power that they work with can be an obstacle to both a Weaver and a ShadowWalker." She gave me a look of warning. "There is a great deal of power. The temptation proved too much for Armando."

The visual her words brought to my mind gave me a sick feeling. "He removed the protection from her."

"Yes." She nodded. "What your grandmother didn't know was that Armando had made a deal with the demon Kine. He was offered great power and influence, and the temptation was too much for him to resist. All he had to do was get Claire out of the way."

"And he knew I wasn't ready to drink from the cup."

"The demon knew. It assured Armando that with Claire out of the way there would be no one to block access to the portal."

"Then why would he want to come after me to get the cup?"

"Power is a great corrupter, but along with power comes fear. The fear that the power can be lost. I believe Armando began to worry that the older you got the more chance there was that you would find out about the cup, and you would take on the role of Michael's ShadowWalker. He believes if he possesses the cup he can prevent that from ever happening."

A thought occurred to me. "Okay, so I drink from the cup. Who weaves for me?"

"That is a question we will have to discuss after you make your decision. But right now, I think the time for that decision has come. Whatever you decide, the rest of us are going to have to deal with. We need the time to do so if your answer is no."

"So I still can say no?"

"Of course. Up until the moment you drink you have that choice."

"What if I'm not up to this? What if I drink and then I can't do what needs to be done?"

"I don't think that's what you really need to know. You've come here looking for answers when the answer is inside you. Most decisions are worked out one step at a time, and this one is no different."

I was pretty sure the only thing inside me was confusion, but I wasn't going to argue the point.

I looked over at Matthias, but he just stared back. "I want to put Eddie back in the ground, stop Vigil from getting the cup, and then I can think about all the other…stuff."

She nodded. "Okay. It's simple."

"You keep saying that, but so far I haven't found anything about any of this that I would call simple."

"That's because you haven't taken the first step."

"The cup?"

"The cup. You must decide what you're going to do. Nothing else can happen until that decision is made. Until the ceremony is done."

"Lots of things have been happening without me making that decision. You told me that the rest of you have been holding the line." *And you haven't yet told me who the rest of you are.* I ignored the voice in my head. "Why is now so different?"

She stared at me with a patient smile. I was really sick of everyone looking at me as if they were waiting for me to catch up. My new friends weren't turning out to be much fun to play with. If I was supposed to be so important to the team, why the hell did I feel like the loser who never got picked every time they looked at me?

"Because it is now."

I shook my head. "Okay, I can't take any more riddles, so I guess it's time for me to surrender."

She rose from her chair and pulled me from the stool. With that clear gaze, she looked me right in the eye.

"Are you ready and willing to drink from the cup of Michael and accept your legacy, Rosalie DeSalvo?"

The cup had only meant a problem for me, a tool that would disrupt the careful life I'd built since my Granny's death. It was the enemy, in some ways, of the Craft I practiced—simple and light—and the open door to a darker world than I was ready for. I had not looked at it as something holy, as the beloved heirloom of an archangel. Maybe it was time for me to truly decide, because if I drank from this cup, I belonged to the world it opened up to me. It was time for me to get off the fence.

I took a deep breath. "Yes. I'm ready."

I felt Matthais' warm hand slip into mine. He wasn't one for comfort, so the gesture made me wonder if my face looked as terrified as I felt inside. When I looked up at him, I thought maybe I had pegged him wrong. There was sympathy in his gaze. Not exactly comforting, but better than a blank stare.

Irene held out a soft black robe I hadn't seen her get.

"You can bathe in there." She jerked her chin toward a small door beside the woodstove.

"Really? I don't think we have time for that. We need to get on with—"

"With the business at hand. Bathe, dress and I will take you to the portal. There you will make your vows to Michael as his ShadowWalker. After you do that, your task will become clearer in your mind."

I started to tell her my task was crystal clear in my

head right now, but she'd already turned and walked away. Matthais nudged me.

"It'll be okay, Rose. Ceremony can be an important component to magick, and you need all the energy you can to take on Vigil."

"And what about Eddie? Time's running out for him."

"Let me worry about Eddie. That's why I'm here, remember?"

Was it really, I thought. *Or are you hiding something else from me?* For a moment I wondered if Matthias was one of the ones holding the line. Was that why he had been willing to come to a stranger's house in the middle of the night?

I heard Irene clear her throat and looked up to find her staring at me. Her gaze shifted to the bathroom door, her meaning clearer than words.

"I'm going."

If I ever got to be this ShadowWalker everyone was so enamored of, I was going to start bossing people around instead of taking orders from every stranger I came across.

A half hour later, I stood in front of a small stone wall hidden behind Irene's house, barefoot and cloaked in the black robe and the soft tunic and pants she had found for me. They fit well, which was another coincidence to wonder about. She had instructed Matthias to stay inside. As she handed me the velvet bag she'd filled with herbs while I bathed, she kissed me on the forehead. Then she placed a long, rather wicked looking blade in my hands. It wasn't quite a sword but definitely more than a knife. I looked at her, and she smiled.

"It might come in handy."

I wanted to believe she was protecting me from snakes and other such normal threats, but my little voice told me to be prepared for anything. Irene reached around me to tie a long strip of leather around my waist, and I slid the blade in the sheath on the side of it when she was done.

"My gift to you, for I cannot go any further with you. This is a walk you must make yourself." She pointed down the dirt path that led to the mountain behind the house. "Walk straight down the path. Sprinkle the herbs along the path as you go. You will see the opening when you get closer. The cup is waiting for you."

That thought wasn't pleasant. I really, really wanted somebody to hold my hand through all this. I was already missing Matthias, his absence making me realize how much I'd depended on him the last few hours. Usually I didn't connect with strangers that easily. Now I felt completely alone and very, very scared.

Not alone.

The familiar voice brought a twinge to my already nervous belly. I felt Granny Claire all around me as her voice whispered on the breeze.

Never alone, Rose.

She'd walked this walk. Done this ceremony. And she had done it alone. At least so far as her family was concerned. None of us had even imagined this as part of her life. As I stepped toward the narrow opening, I knew she went with me, and for the moment that was enough.

Chapter Eighteen

It was cool and damp inside the cavern, and I found myself grateful for the thick robe. Most ritual garb is for looks, not actual use. I hugged the soft fabric against me as I stared around the open space. I stood in what looked like an antechamber, a wide empty space big enough to make the narrow tunnel that led off from it look more than a bit claustrophobic. Unlike Jokyu's domain, the cavern showed no remodeling to accommodate the twenty-first century. Its interior remained as it must have looked for thousands of years, with no modern equipment in sight.

Not that sight was easy to come by. The sunlight faded behind me, and the way in front, while not completely dark, wasn't what I would call well-lit either. *Weren't places like this supposed to have torches on the walls for people to pick up?* I guess if you delay coming when you're supposed to then you don't get to be bitchy about the preparations for your arrival.

I took a cautious step further in, not really enjoying the feel of the loss of a bit more of the sunlight. The rock walls weren't carved, at least not by human hands. Maybe angelic means had brought it into existence, but it seemed more likely it had been hewn by the forces of nature, a creation of some long ago ice age's retreat. The air had that musty smell to it, like the only circulation it got was around and around the same space. I wondered for a moment how many people like me this place had seen. *And how many of them had died here.* That thought gave me a shiver that had nothing to do with the chill in the air. I couldn't help the quick glance around, grateful I didn't see any old bones. Indiana Jones, I am not.

In all my turning my hand bumped the sheath and the weight of its contents against my leg gave me pause. My grandmother had been big on omens and the heavy blade bouncing against me seemed like a freaking neon sign telling me to look out for major life changes ahead. I'm not a weapons girl. I always wanted to be the wizard who throws magickal spells at the villain, not the kick-ass warrior who took them down by hand-to-hand combat. It seemed like I'd been gifted with a frigging destiny that hadn't taken into account any of my own desires. All I kept getting offered was one more change to deal with. I sighed and hugged the robe a little bit closer.

Since my life was going to go to somewhere resembling Hell and I wasn't even sure I got a hand basket for the ride, I opted to take a moment to let myself settle. The silence in the cavern created a void in my senses that had me disoriented. I'd been pretty disoriented for the last few hours anyway, so the addition didn't help at all. Connections were important to me, and other than the knowledge that my beloved grandmother had been here, I didn't have any connections to this space, no memories that could well up in my head and help me adjust to unfamiliar surroundings.

I let my hand slide along the rough walls, trying to

gain some understanding of where I was, and what I would find here. Maybe I was trying to stall for a minute too, but if I was, there was no one around to notice. Or at least I hoped there wasn't.

Not that it mattered. The only thing I got from my exploration was a scrape across my palm. Like everything and everyone else I had encountered over the last few hours, the place appeared to be waiting for me to make my decision before answering any questions. Guess everything really did hinge on my answer to the most important question waiting. Self-sacrifice must be the key to all of it.

Tiny droplets of blood welled up under my skin, and I had a thought. Maybe it was some sort of innate knowledge meant to guide me and maybe it was just me being my normal overly dramatic self, but I squeezed the skin of my palm together to get a bit more of the blood to the surface. Then I placed my hand against the cavern wall once more.

My answer was immediate. Heat pooled beneath my skin, changing the cool stone to a rock of fire that soaked up the blood as if it were fuel. I tried not to wince. No matter how bad I wanted to pull my hand away, I understood now that an offering needed to be made, and my blood was a satisfactory one. The second message was if this place was to become mine in any way, I couldn't flinch from doing what needed to be done. My days of denial had to be behind me or my tenure as a ShadowWalker was going to be pretty short. After a minute the burning sensation eased, and the cool chill of the stone returned. Something settled in my spirit as I moved away from the wall that had fed from me. With a prayer of thanks, I lowered my hand and turned to follow the narrow path to my destiny, whatever it might be.

I'd walked for only a few minutes when I rounded the corner into another antechamber. A shaft of sunlight beamed down from an opening in the rock far above, tiny dust mites shining in it like diamonds floating down from heaven. Their landing spot looked anything but celestial though. The light illuminated the small pool at the back of the cavern, not altogether a good thing as the water in it looked anything but inviting.

More cautious than curious, I stepped toward the silent pool. The water lay in a circle of stone about five feet around. Big enough to drown someone in, I thought, then wondered if the sudden homicidal tendencies came from the dark energy I could feel drifting along the edge of the water. It curled around the stone crevices like smoke from an open grill, spoiling the whole picture I'd drawn in my head of this moment. In spite of the image of a collection of shadows and darkness that the story on the scroll had created, my imagination had visualized it as a bubbling spring of fresh waters. I had so hoped for something clear and crystalline and pure. Boundless optimism is my middle name. Chalk another one up for the dream crusher.

The reality lay still and motionless against its rough stone border, looking exactly like the scroll had depicted it. A glance down into its depths showed me nothing. The surface of the water resembled black tar, dark and murky and about a ten on my creepy scale. It smelled strong enough to make me want to gag, a stagnant, gross odor that held hints of unpleasant things living below the dark scum on top.

I swallowed the lump of bile stuck in my throat.

My stomach tried to refuse the delivery. It had sent it up once and clearly had a no return policy. Hoping it wouldn't get me in trouble for being offensive to my angelic ancestor, I bent over and spit it out of my mouth. My reaction didn't bode well for my job skills. If the mere sight of the pool could make me puke, I had to wonder how I was going to get a cupful down to my uncooperative stomach. Get a grip, Rose, I thought, it's just water. Or at least I hoped so. Now would not be a good time for some monster to be trying to make its entrance through the portal. Then I glanced to my right, and there it was.

The cup sat in a niche in the wall, a tiny ray from the sun illuminating its resting place. It looked like all that was light and open and honest, and the beauty of it shone like gold across the dark pool. My fingers tingled with magickal energy as I reached for it then pulled back. I stepped closer and looked at it, really looked at the carving and the intricate detail on the outside. There were words on the inside as well, that I hadn't seen in the drawing. I picked it up, warmed at once by the feel of it against my skin. If the pool had brought fear, the cup brought peace, an odd quality since it was the cup that would bring such turmoil to my life should I drink from it. I traced one finger over the words carved inside. *In umbra, vires.* The Latin drilled into me through eight years of Catholic school came through. *In shadow, strength.*

My hand wrapped carefully around the cup, afraid I might drop it. Something told me there could definitely be some cosmic repercussions from breaking Michael's cup. Once I held it, though, I realized the cup was anything but fragile. Its appearance made it look delicate and all too breakable. The magick thrumming through it let me know it wasn't. The palm of my hand where the blood was smeared brushed against the carved faces, and I felt a sigh against my skin. *Had they been waiting for me all these years, too?* I could only hope I had time to catch up on all the things I didn't know. Having my name go down as the biggest failure in the history of ShadowWalkers was not a pleasant thought.

Knowledge was power, Matthias had lectured me. Now knowledge bloomed inside me, bringing with it a surety and a confidence I knew had never been mine before. I leaned over the surface of the pool.

"In shadow, strength."

I murmured the phrase as I dipped the cup into the murky water, and the sighs echoed around me. The words felt like a cloak shielding me as I lifted the cup to my lips. I should have taken that as a warning about what was coming, but my boundless optimism struck again. The dark water burned all the way down my throat, the slimy feel of it in my mouth acrid and painful. Part of me wanted to spit it back out, but some latent sensibility told me that wouldn't be a good idea. I didn't want the stuff going back over my lips a second time. With a sheer strength of will I thought must have come from the words, I swallowed, hoping the foul liquid didn't burn a hole in my stomach. Strength, hell, it would take a mouth made of steel to not be bothered by that.

The magick must have extended all the way inside me for my picky stomach held onto the contents. It wasn't happy, but it kept it down. With the last of it past my throat, I put the cool cup against my forehead and waited for my stomach to stop roiling. As I did, I felt the weight of the cup in my hand. Guess I'd gotten an answer to at least one of my questions, and it so wasn't the answer I'd hoped for. I glanced at the cup, wondering if there was a way to just wish it gone. *Did I have that kind of power now?* Even as I thought it, I knew the answer was no. Whatever else lay ahead, I was still in a very vulnerable position so long as the cup decided to stick around. Good to know I had one more problem to solve just as soon as I got the time. Of course, my death would be a solution, but it wasn't the one I preferred.

It was becoming clear I had other problems as well. Walking in here, I'd had the idea that my eyes would zoom in immediately on what lay in the shadows as soon as the cup left my lips, and I wanted to be prepared for anything creepy to show up right away. Like the last few hours, the bad things didn't disappoint me. They showed up in spades.

I zeroed in on the fact that I could hear things and see things that hadn't been there when I came in as soon as I opened my eyes. Or if they'd been there I hadn't noticed them. All around me I heard the murmurs of things past and present, echoes left behind from all the dark thoughts of those who had passed through the portal. The feeling reminded me of the people on the cup. I wondered if it was an omen of what my life would be like now. Would the voices haunt me? I shook off the thought and tried to focus instead on what the next step would be.

The smoky darkness lifted from the edge of the pool to float around the air above it like an evil serpent. Whispers of voices echoed through it as it danced along the rock walls. If what I heard now was any indication, there was a lot of dark magick floating around this space. Not just floating, it had made itself at home in this land. In my land. The dark had claimed my little corner of the world, using it as a veritable buffet for its own gorging.

Something about the thought of my world and the people in it being dinner for the kind of evil I felt here made my stomach settle, its turmoil replaced by anger of a most righteous kind. I embraced the rage building inside me, absorbing its energy into my spirit like armor. If I had any chance of accomplishing this task, the fury I felt was going to have to become my good friend. I was going to have to learn how to tap into its energy when I needed it. The feel of it inside me now made a fire in my belly. I closed my eyes and visualized those flames burning their way down through my body, flowing through my heart and out to my arms, my legs, my fingers and my toes. I welcomed it with a chant of gratitude my grandmother had taught me, letting the hot feel of it shape itself like armor over every part of my physical and my ethereal body. My guess was its presence was the celestial equivalent of pinning on the marshal's badge. I could go forth now, duly deputized in my new kick-ass capacity. It couldn't hurt to be official, I thought. Maybe there would be some unexpected back-up along the way.

With newfound strength, I lifted my face to the pool. The water now looked clear and crystalline and pure. Oh, now you clear up, I thought and you probably taste like mountain spring water. Somehow my willingness to down a cup of toxic sludge had changed things. Guess sacrifice is supposed to come with some discomfort, although I thought it might take a while for me and my stomach to be on good terms again.

"Well, is it all you wished for, ShadowWalker?"

My fingers tightened on the cup as I whirled around to find the source of the voice. Then my jaw almost dropped to the ground as I stared at Yvette. She stood behind me like a vision of an old nightmare, D-cups and all, but now she was dressed in what looked like a gown of blood, the deep red shimmer of it clinging to her body in a macabre waterfall. Her feet were bare, and all that red hair flowed around her, melting into the red of the gown. I found myself glad Eddie wasn't with me because the gown fit her like a glove, and there were a few things it fit so tight they were popping out.

What hadn't changed was her expression. Her face held the same smirk I remembered as she stalked toward me with a predatory stride that had anger rising back up in me. I didn't know where she fit into this yet, but the hungry look on her face made my blood boil. I wasn't anybody's dinner, a fact I looked forward to making Little Red Riding Hood aware of just as soon as I figured out how this whole ShadowWalker thing worked. Which I hoped was really, really soon.

"I see you found your toy." She nodded at the cup still clenched in my hand. "You must be feeling pretty powerful right about now." With a sensual move, she stretched her arms out and smiled. "Umm, power. It's addicting, isn't it? The real thing, not the pitiful excuse for it that humanity settles for."

Yvette licked her lips, her voice a low purr that sent an echo of sheer lust through the deep cavern. And through me. I wouldn't have thought anything short of mind-blowing sex would have gotten me that hot, but her words pelted my insides with the white fire of need. My mouth went dry as I stared at her. I could tell from the look in her eyes she knew what I was thinking, knew the effect her words were having on me. Something told me I needed to start kicking ass soon or I'd be just a puddle on the floor.

"And you've only gotten a small taste so far. Just wait, little ShadowWalker, until you've felt that power coursing through your veins for a decade, for longer. Until it becomes more familiar to you than anything else, and you crave its elixir above all other things." She tilted her head and frowned. "Oh, that's right. You aren't going to be around long enough for that. Oh, that's too bad."

My brain still worked enough to let me know she wasn't broken up over the thought, but my mouth was still too dry to spit anything out. I clutched the cup a bit tighter as I stood there, hoping some witty remark would force its way out. This had been a long journey through the unexpected and seeing her here fit that theme all too well. Had Vigil sent her to follow me and take the cup, I wondered. She tsked at me, tossing all the red hair around with a pouty look on her lips.

"What, still got a mouthful of holy water? No snotty remarks to make about all the things you're going to do to me now that you're the One, the all-powerful ShadowWalker anointed by Michael?"

"You?" My mouth finally caught up with my eyes enough to croak out that one word. Yvette? Here? "What are you doing here?" I glanced back at the entrance then back to her. "How did you get in here?"

A moment of panic about Irene and the others

bubbled up in my throat, but I swallowed it down. Yvette appeared to be alone, and I didn't think she could have taken both Irene and Matthias on her own.

"How did you even know where this place was?" As soon as the question left my mouth, I realized how stupid it was. Of course she knew. She knew a hell of a lot more than I did.

"Unlike you, I belong here. My destiny has never been in question."

The words held a venom that matched the bitch I remembered. Her eyes held the same contempt, the same desire to see me suffer too, only this time they weren't human eyes at all. They glowed an eerie red, like a hot burning coal. My estimation of my discernment abilities took a tumble. Whatever she was, she wasn't human, at least not all the way. I managed not to take a step back as she got closer. It didn't help. The hate spitting out of those red eyes could have burned me at a thousand paces.

"This is my place. I should be the one asking what you're doing here. Or the one kicking your ass out of here."

"But…" I tried not to stammer. "You have no magick. Nothing. I didn't feel anything coming from you." *Well, nothing except hate.*

She snorted. "And you are going to be their savior, the great guardian of the Portal of Ornias. Yet you do not even understand the rules of the game. Magick? No, there is nothing so primitive as your pitiful concept of magick in my blood. I have the power of the Archangels in my blood, a power I have used and respected since my making. Unlike certain others." She gave me such a look of disdain I felt it hit me like a blow.

I understood then, as the smear of her words and the hate they carried slimed across my spirit. Yvette was a child of the Fallen. Angel, yes, but dark angel according to Michael's scroll. Well, didn't this take the cake, I thought. D-cups and a demon inside. *Talk about the child who got everything.*

That thought had me feeling a little left out of the inheritance, which didn't bode well for the fight that lay ahead of me. Nothing like hitting the ground running, I decided, as I did a quick inventory of what I did have. My inventory didn't take long because it consisted mostly of simple magick and stubbornness. Now if I could only figure out a way to use those two things that would make Jokyu eat his words about how woefully unprepared I was. Not that he was wrong. I just wanted to survive long enough to make him eat his words. The thought almost made me smile.

As for the matter at hand, I focused my attention on the monster all dressed up in front of me. *And wasn't she an unexpected addition to the mix.* I was getting more than a little tired of everyone around me springing surprises on me at the last minute, mostly because they were never the pleasant kind. It was time I tapped into some of the anger that had been building up in me over the last few hours. To start things rolling, I fell back on my old standby, sarcasm.

"Wow, did you think of all those insults all by yourself or are you still letting Vigil put words in your mouth? Your delivery of them was excellent, by the way. You might even be worth the money he's paying you."

Her hand lifted in a flash, and I just had time to

catch it before the blow struck my face. We played a short game of arm wrestling before she jerked her arm back. I let it go, unhappy at how strong she'd turned out to be, but grateful for my dad's obsession with arm wrestling. I could only hope she hadn't figured out how strong I wasn't from it. Her pretty lips curled into a sneer.

"How dare you! No one puts words in my mouth, least of all a human whose very existence is to be food for those he serves."

Baiting her seemed to work better than wrestling with her, so I decided to stick with it. This time I was the one doing the tsking.

"And by those he serves I assume you mean yourself?" I gave her a look of wide-eyed disbelief. "That's just kind of hard to swallow, sorry. The idea that you're the power in his game, I mean. It's a tough sell. From what I saw, it was pretty much the other way around. Although, I have to admit, if that's the truth, then you're some kind of actress."

This time I gave her what I hoped could be taken as an appreciative smile.

"Excuse me?" Her gaze never left me as I moved closer, but her fingers curled up like claws.

"You're telling me you're the one in charge, the better half. You want me to believe that you're the power behind Vigil's throne, and you allow him to talk to you like his little lapdog because that's all part of the act. He ordered you around like his errand girl. Must have sucked to have to play that part when you're the one who feeds him that power."

Her pretty face melted into a snarl. "I am no one's dog."

"Sorry, I thought putting it that way might be nicer than saying bitch. My mom once washed my mouth out with soap for calling this girl in my homeroom class that word. But, I guess if the shoe fits, *bitch*. And now it gets worse, 'cause it isn't only Vigil who gets to order you around. Now you have to leave this spot and get out of town because I'm here. That's gotta hurt too. I'd say it's humans two, Yvette zero."

This time she laughed. My hope that I could put off till another time the ass-kicking started to fade a bit. *Who are you kidding, Rose? There's no way she's just gonna walk away.*

"I suppose you think your wit and your smart mouth will take the place of the true strength of a ShadowWalker. Oh, but wait, that's all you have, isn't it? You've had no training, no preparation. You are, what is it you humans call it, a sitting duck? A weak, helpless animal that is prey for anything that comes along."

She took another step closer as she fixed me with a glare of pure hate. "I have no intention of leaving. This is my place, I have claimed it, and unlike you, I have the power to hold it."

I stared her down, ignoring everything but the years of frustration pent up in me at my treatment by pretty girls like her who thought they owned the world. Didn't know that was in my arsenal, but I was sure going to use it.

"Well, change of plans, bitch. Your baggage claim ticket is no longer valid." I was starting to enjoy the use of the b-word. For some reason using it made me feel really powerful. Who knew a simple cuss word would be my weapon of choice at a time like this?

"And here's something else you can stuff into that pretty head of yours. I have the authority, which means the balance of power has shifted, too. I'm here now. I'm Michael's ShadowWalker, and that makes you the unwelcome visitor with a ticket out of here."

She moved fast, and I discovered another addition to my arsenal. I could move fast, too. As soon as she grabbed me by the front of the robe, I had Irene's blade pressed against her chest.

"Let. Go. Or I deflate a boob."

I growled the words at her, surprised to see her smile in return. That couldn't be good. Before I could fulfill my dream of making her an A cup, her fingers relaxed their grip. I kept the blade where it was. Hey, if she didn't like it she could step back. She looked down to it and then back up to me. Her voice dripped with contempt when she spoke.

"Did you really think that was all it would take when you drank from that stupid cup? You say go and we all walk away, terrified of the great and mighty ShadowWalker, helpless before your mighty power. Are you that simple-minded?"

Nasty didn't begin to cover the look on her face. Part of me longed to tell her she could say what she wanted, that I wasn't insulted. I loved simple. My whole life had been simple up till this moment. Oh, it had its bumps and jolts, but overall simple had been my middle name up till now. That was particularly true with my magick. This new, more complicated me was having a bit of trouble understanding that simple had gone out of my life. My gaze caught the fire-red of her eyes, and I changed my mind. This was going to be simple. Like it or not she had to go. I straightened my shoulders and stared her down.

"I have read the scroll, and I know who wins this one. Guess you didn't read the memo. I'm here now, and you get to leave. That's how simple it's going to be."

This time she did step back. I kept the blade up and ready. She looked down, but it wasn't the blade that caught her eye. Her gaze was glued to the cup still gripped in my hand. I shifted it behind me. For some reason I didn't want her staring at it.

"Mine." I said it quietly but with a thread of steel to my voice.

"Yes, but for how long?"

"Longer than you're going to be around, that much I know."

"I doubt that."

She stalked around me, haughty and defiant. Guess when you look like she did you get used to being the queen. Although, the thought did occur to me to wonder if what I saw was her true image. Something to think about for later. I turned with her, step by step, pretty sure I didn't want to take my eyes off her for a nanosecond.

"You turn your back on what you are for years and in one little drink you call the power of the Ancients to come into an untrained body of pitiful flesh and bone and expect to be respected for it. You have not earned this. You don't deserve it."

"Sticks and stones." I shrugged. "That's the thing about family, you know? Some of us get the good genes, and some of us don't."

She growled at me. Not at all the sound I was expecting, and from the look on her face, it wasn't all she wanted to do either. I shook my head at her, keeping my voice light and a smile plastered on my face.

"Look, we can stand here all night talking dysfunctional family stuff or you can go back through the portal like a good little monster, Yvette. Or should I call you that? Maybe you go by something else when you're not playing the servant."

"Maybe I will leave your bones here by this water for the rats to find. Perhaps, though, even they will not be interested in a meal of one who is as stupid as you must be to think I would give you the power of my name."

She was breathing hard, but other than that, she hadn't made a move toward me. Which had me wondering why? If I kept pushing would she break? If she broke, could I take her? Ah, the questions were piling up, and I was running on a tight schedule. This was so not the way I had envisioned the aftermath of my ceremony. Where was the cake, the flowers?

"I'll stick with Yvette then. Guess we don't really know each other well enough for nicknames. Like I said, there's this thing about family. You can go your whole life not knowing someone and bam, one day you find out you're descended from an angel. Or rather an archangel. They're the more important ones, right?"

"And you think that entitles you to respect? That the name of Michael makes you powerful?" She stopped circling and got up in my face again. This time, though, she kept her hands to herself.

"In your arrogance you sit without a plate at a feast I can taste only in my dreams. You call upon a power you have no knowledge of and cloak yourself in a magick you have ignored for years. Why are you here now?"

Jokyu's words came back to me, almost the same ones as the monster in front of me taunted me with. I lifted the blade up.

"I'm not ignoring it anymore. And I'm here to tell you to get the hell back where you belong."

"Why should the spawn of Michael be invited to the richness of such a banquet while my brethren and I starve on the crumbs that are left? Why should such a weak, pathetic thing as you be handed power while we must scrape and scrounge for it?"

I shook my head as I watched her for any sudden moves. Being a smartass was one thing. When it came time to get physical I wanted all the warning I could get.

"Like I said, that's the sucky part about family. Some get it and some don't. Just the way it goes. I don't really have an answer for why."

"You have answers for very little, human."

She had me there, but I wasn't about to let her know it. Pretty much all I really had were questions. A whole lot of questions. Since I hadn't gotten a whole lot of answers from anyone else, I thought, what the hell, why not go to the source?

"You've got me there. Answers haven't exactly been rushing my way. Maybe I've been asking the wrong people. So just what are you, Yvette, a puppet? A puppetmaster? Do you get to pull any strings or is your reward just shits and giggles?"

She stepped back and shook all that red hair out as she stretched and gave a lazy yawn before putting her hands on her hips.

"What I am is bored with this game. Since you appear to be so eager to test your newfound power, I should let you do it. I have other things to see to so let's cut our little visit short. That way I can get back to what is more important to me."

Okay, I guess now things were going to get physical. Yvette did look bored, but I hoped I could chalk that up to overconfidence. I wasn't known for being a fighter, not even in high school. My dad once said I was more of a scrapper than a fighter, more like a badger. I grabbed on and didn't let go. The only problem with that now was if I grabbed her I knew I would very much want to let go of Yvette. How much effort it would take to tumble her back into the water was the question. More questions, I thought.

While I was busy plotting strategy in my head, I happened to notice that Yvette hadn't moved. She hadn't taken a fighting stance, hell even her hands were no longer balled up into fists. If she could've been any more relaxed I didn't know how. I had a really bad feeling that once again I was missing a very important answer. When she smirked at me the bad feeling got worse.

"Do you think I'm just going to let you walk by me?" I gripped the blade tighter.

"I think you're going to be too busy to do much of anything else." She smiled like she had all the time in the world. "My brother has been looking forward to meeting you."

She waved a hand in the general direction of behind me, and I wanted to snort. I sure wasn't going to buy the old "there's someone behind you" routine. Then I heard the growl, and this time it wasn't coming out of Yvette's mouth. Must be a family trademark, I thought.

My whole body went rigid at the sound. *Did I dare turn and look?* My inner voice took to yelling to get my attention as it screamed at me not to turn my head. I knew it was probably right because everything inside me told me I so didn't want to see what was back there. What was going on in front of me wasn't really what I wanted to see either. Yvette moved way inside my personal space boundary to get right up in my face.

"Nothing like getting to know the whole family, is there, dear Rose?"

She smirked as she walked past me, tilting her head to look behind me as she spoke.

"Don't forget the cup when you're done."

I let my gaze follow her. Keeping the monster you know in sight sounded like a good plan, even when the one you didn't know was making nasty noises behind you. My fingers curled around the cup at her words. Now there was some incentive to make the effort, I thought. Even if I died right here, right now, the cup would stay, waiting for whoever was in line behind me. The sad part was it would never reach that person. The cup, and all the power that went with it, would land right in the greedy, murderous fingers of Armando Vigil. One drink had put me past the time when I could give it anything besides my best shot. I was the hope of the world now, at least of my little part of it. It was win or allow the whole world to get screwed. No pressure.

Whatever it was behind me growled again. Guess brother dearest didn't like being ignored. The sound brought my attention back to the whole dying here and now thing, a vocal reminder of the fact I shouldn't let that happen. I didn't jump, but I did do a slow turn that let me see Yvette walk out the entrance before I turned away completely to face the new threat. It was a good thing I didn't turn fast for as soon as I got halfway around, the room started spinning and my whole world shifted on its axis.

I wasn't quite sure where I was, but my new location didn't look a thing like the old one. For one thing it was really, really dark. And it wasn't the kind of night-sky, beautiful moonlight, let's look at the starry heavens kind of dark. This was the somebody threw a blanket over me and is now trying to suffocate me kind of dark. I couldn't even see my hand in front of my face, which meant I probably wasn't going to see anything coming at me either. And something told me there were things I didn't want coming at me unaware in this dark.

I did have room to run though, or at least the new space felt that open. The new expanse seemed like a contradiction to the threatening feel of the darkness all around me. Not that I could see where I was going if I did choose to run. The confined feeling of the cavern was gone, replaced by the sensation of endless nothingness. It might have felt less threatening if not for the distinct sensation of having fallen out of a safe container into a bottomless well. As if there were no walls to protect me anymore, nothing around me to catch me when I got thrown. From the way it felt, I was lost in space, without air, without memory, without hope of ever landing anywhere firm and solid again. Without hope of coming out of this space alive. Even the ground beneath me felt spongy, as if it might give way at any moment.

I kept blinking my eyes, as if that would help them adjust to the sudden absence of light. Part of me wanted to put out my hands and try to shove the suffocating feeling away from me. I knew it was silly, knew there was air around me for I was still breathing. My brain did a quick flashback to Jokyu and the mountain, but I gulped in a breath and felt the air go down my lungs. Wherever I was, I could breathe. I just had to figure out what to do to make sure that continued to happen.

Almost as soon as I got my breath under control, the creepy factor shot up into the nether realms. Something was watching me. Something my newfound spidey senses told me was more than a little unfriendly. I moved my head in a slow arc, trying to take in any shapes or movements around me as I reminded myself that I had those new senses, and it would probably be a good thing to use them. I stood still again and closed my eyes. It was a risk, but I needed to calm myself. If I was going to die here, it wouldn't be without trying every trick I had in my book. Maybe it was earth beneath me and maybe it wasn't, but my power could still be grounded in my own center and that's what I did.

In spite of my efforts, I wasn't prepared for what hit me. My visions had all involved the physical, with me getting my ass handed to me by something ten times my size. What hadn't occurred to me was having my psyche handed to me by something ten times as evil as I was. But a nasty something rolled over my mind like a runaway train, shattering all the grounding I'd done like it was nothing but empty air. My brain started rattling off distress signals to the rest of me, and my heart rate shot through the roof as every fear I'd ever had blossomed into full-blown reality in the darkness around me. Sounds that hadn't been there before whispered in my ear, and the shadows held dark and fearful shapes that moved closer and closer to where I stood.

Thirty seconds after whatever it was hit me, I was so cold my teeth started chattering. Even though I told myself it wasn't possible, I felt as if all human warmth had been sucked out of me. Tears welled in my eyes as a voice in my head told me I had no hope, no chance, no reason to even try getting away from my impending doom. Nothingness folded around me like a towel, wiping away everything I held dear, every reason I had said yes to this path. My doom wasn't impending, it was here, and I had nothing to fight it with and no reason to believe I could escape it.

My heart beat so fast I thought it might fly out of my chest. Stark terror beat down everything else struggling inside me. I thought I'd been scared before, but it was nothing like this. Even the whole deal of finding Eddie hadn't inscribed the kind of traumatic horror now writing itself on my spirit. I felt the air on my face but couldn't seem to get it down into my lungs. If I could have, I knew I would be screaming. The silence gathered around me like an enemy, laughing at the fact my terror couldn't even make itself known in the dark. I whirled around and around, looking for something, anything to explain the naked fear filling me like water overflowing an empty glass. All I saw was darkness. My whole world was darkness and the weight of it drowned me.

I swallowed hard, tried to focus my scattered energy. It was more of an effort than I wanted to admit to get a grip on the thoughts rolling through my head. The litany of doom and destruction had a mind of its own and a determination to set my own mind adrift in its sea of despair. I would capture a moment of calm only to find it yanked away from me by my own thoughts.

Then as swiftly as it came the feeling was gone. My knees folded, and my body collapsed from the sudden change. I hit hard ground as I dropped and wanted to kiss it. Air flooded my lungs as my heart slowed to its normal rhythm and the world around me stopped spinning. A dim light glowed in the distance, enough for me to see a few feet in front of me. To my surprise it looked like I was still in the cavern. For a moment I could only sit there, trying to catch both my breath and my equilibrium. Before I could get a firm grip on either one, a chuckle echoed off the stone walls around me.

I'd been laughed at a lot in my life so I knew the sound of that kind of chuckle. This sound was like the source, the wellspring of that kind of bullying laughter. It held all the malice, disgust, and outright hatred that fed bullies everywhere.

"Did I frighten you, little ShadowWalker?" Disdain oozed from the disembodied voice. "It is hard to walk in the shadows when you are scared of the dark, is it not?"

The voice was deep, with a strange tone that made the hairs on my neck tingle. It resonated in the space with an energy that made the temperature of the room rise several degrees. I rose to my feet, getting steadier by the minute as I grounded myself again. The adrenaline rushing through my system slowed, but I pumped it back up, knowing I needed the energy boost. There was enough of it left that I felt my heart rate speed up again. Only this time I was the one controlling it. Alexis taught me that temper and memory are both wonderful tools so long as you retain control of them. And I planned on using them to put an end to this fight right now. No one and nothing was going to bully me again. Not now. Not ever. At least not and walk away from it without some damage of their own.

"I'm not scared now, so why don't you come out of the shadows and face me." I issued the challenge with a whole lot more confidence than I felt, but I'd never known a bully it was safe to back down from. If I got beat up at least I'd be standing up when it started.

"Ah, bravery. The human antidote to fear. If I remember correctly, now I am to cower and tremble at your courage. Isn't that the way it works, little ShadowWalker?"

"Now you leave. I don't care if you cower or tremble, so long as you do it on your way out of here and back to whatever slime pit you crawled out of."

"Your words are filled with great confidence and disdain, yet I hear your heart beating so fast. I smell your fear all around you, like the secret flavoring of a special dish. Emotions add such a delightful spice. It always pleases me to welcome a human to my playground for I have found that humans are such emotional creatures."

Amusement tinged the strange energy in his voice. I'll show you emotional, I thought. I would gladly hand him the emotions I felt right now, the ones bordering on the murderous side.

"You want emotion then you're going to love what

I have in mind. Emotional is something I do really well. But I wouldn't get too excited about it if I were you. Not all emotions are fun ones. As a matter of fact, some of them lead to things like death and dismemberment. You know, good old-fashioned violence, things like that."

Laughter wasn't the response I was going for, but it rolled out of him at my words, echoing off the walls. It pissed me off that he clearly felt I was a joke.

"Ah, I hear your words, dear Rose, but I do not believe it is violence which motivates you. You are such a tiny thing, so delicate and so…fragile. So very human. Violence would not become you. I believe I know something which may suit you better for I have been studying you a long time in preparation for our initial confrontation. So long that I had begun to believe we would never have this chance to play."

"Sorry to keep you waiting, but here I am."

"Yes, the opportunity to introduce you to my games has come at last."

"I didn't come here to play games."

"But that is what I do. It seemed you did not like my last one so perhaps this one will suit you better."

I started to throw a shield up but his power hit me before I could. And it hit me in a totally unexpected place. Straight on lust crawled up my insides, burning its way through every nerve ending in my body. Consumed by a depth of desire I hadn't known possible, I lay on the ground, writhing and trying really hard not to scream. My fists pounded against the dirt in a vain attempt to slake the need to touch myself in places I wasn't prepared to expose in public. I was hot all over, the most sensitive parts of my flesh curled around a kind of desire that went beyond any fantasy I'd ever had. I wanted to consume that lust in ways I was sure I had never had the imagination for. And nothing was off limits. Vivid images of skin, of flesh, of violent, pounding sex assaulted my mind, and they included sound and living color. They also included me. In them I did things I wasn't sure were anatomically possible, but my head was thrown back as I moaned and groaned with pleasure. There was blood involved along with the burning sensation of complete and utter abandon as my body rode waves of sexual fulfillment that should have drowned me.

My fingers curled in the dirt, digging deep for something to hold on to while I tried to get some form of shield around my mind. It wasn't easy to do while viewing the clear and potent picture of my mouth doing things it had only dreamed of to a hot naked guy who looked more than willing to let me have my way with him. My sexual buttons hadn't been pushed this hard in a whole lot of years, and my brain was reluctant to take their fun away from them. I promised them we'd explore some of these ideas if we lived through this. They still seemed reluctant to turn away from the sight in front of them, but at last I formed the clear sheet of crystal I used during my meditations. The bright translucent glow of the crystal blocked the images from my sight although it still took several minutes to stop my panting and get my breath under control.

"Bravo, little ShadowWalker. You are a bit stronger than my sister believes you to be."

"I'm a hell of a lot stronger than your bitch of a sister believes me to be." The words might have sounded more confident if my breath still hadn't had a hitch in it. "That's something you both should be careful of."

"Being careful takes all the fun out of things."

I got to my feet, happy when I didn't wobble. "Well, your fun's over now. It's time for you to go."

"I think not. I have been here a long time, and I have decided that this place suits me. It is my playground, and I prefer to stay."

The smooth voice still held a trace of amusement, which pissed me off.

"Playtime's over. You didn't follow the rules, so I really don't give a shit what your preference is. We're going to do things my way now, which means you do what I want."

"Perhaps I was mistaken in my assessment of your penchant for violence after all. I had thought you would wish to avoid a physical confrontation of the more violent kind at all costs, considering your lack of training and aptitude for it. Yet your words call it forth."

"That seems like a longwinded way to call me incompetent and weak. Man, you sure are wordy. Guess we differ in that respect 'cause I only need two words to let you know what I think. Fuck you."

"Oh, and they are such strong words. I should be so afraid."

"I'm thinking you already are since you won't even show your face to me. You hide behind the darkness, playing your little games and running your mouth instead of coming out and facing me. That must mean you're a coward."

"I do not hide in the darkness, little ShadowWalker. I am the darkness. I did you a kindness by not showing myself to you, though you do not seem to know it. You do appear to have a taste for violence after all. Surprising in one of Michael's weak seed."

"Enough with the philosophizing. Come out, come out whatever you are."

One lesson I never seem to learn is not to get cocky in situations I don't have control of. The words had only just left my mouth when he materialized right in front of me. One look and I wished for the darkness again.

He was tall, very, very tall and wide in a muscled bulky sort of way. Standing nearly to the rock ceiling, he towered over me without even trying to intimidate. Both of us knew he had the physical power to crush me without trying hard.

At one time he must have been beautiful for his features were strong and handsome, his presence commanding. Hair the color of the shadows he cloaked himself in hung to his shoulders, and his shoulders were broad. If one looked past the damage done to his looks, he rated far higher on the angelic scale than I did.

His eyes glowed with an amber flame that made the rest of his marred features look as if they had been sacrificed to the fire. It was difficult to tell with what was left of his face, but his features must have been finely chiseled and his skin smooth before whatever had chosen to warp his beauty into a mask of horror had gotten hold of him. Once he must have brought the kind of desire he had foisted on me to every female who saw him. Once.

But the artist who sculpted him must have slipped into madness after his creation for the beauty of his face and body had been destroyed by what looked like acid, leaving a molten ruin of the creature he should have been. That ruin left the shadow of beauty marred by evil for every movement, every sensual line of his violated body oozed an inner malice more threatening than any of the shadows around me. Malevolence radiated off him in waves that threatened to drown me here in the desert sand.

"Are you not pleased to see me, ShadowWalker? You have called me into your presence, and I have come. See the great power you wield."

I tried not to gape, figuring it would be rude. Not that he hadn't been more than rude since we met, but I wanted to do things as easy as possible, at least until they couldn't be easy anymore.

"So, okay, now we've met. I don't think we need any more time to get to know each other. Time for you to go."

"I think not."

The fact that his answer was short, and to the point, afforded me a quick flash of warning before he lashed out at me. Guess playtime was over. This time there were no mind games. It was all physical. He moved like he was born doing martial arts, his whole body rolling with power and energy. His fingers stretched out to reveal hard, black claws, lethal and headed straight for my throat. I ducked and dodged each blow through sheer adrenaline, but sooner or later I'd have to come up with something more than defensive moves if I planned to walk out of here. Each strike he aimed at me was meant to kill. I had no doubt about that.

The next time I stepped back I stumbled, dropping the cup as I struggled not to fall. It rolled behind me, and I moved forward, hoping he hadn't seen it tumble out of my hand. I didn't think he had because his dark gaze was fixed on me as he moved constantly. I ducked and rolled away from where the cup fell, shrugging out of Irene's soft robe as fast as I could. I kicked it back toward the cup, hoping its darkness would cover it. My boundless optimism reared its head again as I managed to convince myself the cup would somehow be hidden from him, kept out of his reach no matter what happened to mc.

Remembering what little self-defense knowledge my dad had been able to pound into my head, I bobbed and weaved each time he came at me. He swiped a claw, catching me on the shoulder, and I went tumbling among the sharp rocks on the floor. I had a second to lay there, stunned and bleeding before he came at me again. The thought occurred to me as I rolled away from him that perhaps defense wasn't what I needed to worry about. If I spent my time defending myself, I had no illusions as to which one of us would tire first, especially since I was already panting, and he didn't look like he'd broken a sweat. Like it or not, it was either kill him or let him kill me. Too bad Dad never covered the offensive side of things. If this became a contest of fighting expertise, the portal was going to be a swinging door that just might hit me in the ass on my way out it.

A clear image of my impending death put some focus back into my movements. That and the desire to get away from the dark magick that poured from him. I saw his lips moving as his body whirled in its killing dance, certain that some of the words were Latin. I had a catch phrase too, I thought, as I murmured the words once more, in umbra, vires. Now if only I had a weapon to go with those words. As soon as I thought it I wanted to smack myself in the head. Visualization. I was really good at visualization.

I didn't dare close my eyes nor did I stop dodging his blows, but in my head I saw myself, armored and armed like my very own version of an angelic knight. Once the image was fixed in my head, I said the words again, louder and stronger this time. As I did I felt cold steel bump against my hand. I had forgotten all about Irene's blade. Always good to know the magick words, I thought. Now if I could figure out more of the super powers that came with this job, it was within the realm of possibility that I wouldn't spend my time as a one-night-stand of a ShadowWalker after all.

He came at me again, hitting my shoulder with what felt like the power of a small tank, and before I knew it, the blade and I parted company. So much for my visualization. In between my huffing and puffing, I racked my brain for any of the binding or banishing spells I knew. I needed help and I needed it now. It didn't appear any of my wild blows had touched him while I had blood dripping in my eyes.

Magick on the fly was my strong point, but something told me I'd have to get even better at it. There were a whole lot of things I was going to be practicing just as soon as somebody or something wasn't out to kill me. Judging by the last few hours, my practice time was going to have to be intense because it didn't look like there was going to be a lot of it. Hell, I'd only been at this ShadowWalker thing for an hour or so and I was ready for retirement. Jokyu sure wouldn't miss me. He'd probably be happy to be proven right about how useless I was. There had to be someone else waiting in the wings, didn't there? With my luck that person was a small child, and there was no one to step into the job now. Everyone would be mad at me for not saving the world. I dropped to the ground just as his momentum carried him forward, pleased to see him tumble over the spot where I'd been. With him distracted for the moment, I reached for the blade. This time I gripped it like the lifesaver it was. His tumble had been far more elegant than mine, as was his recovery. He rolled back up to his feet just as I managed to stand, blade out in front of me. He smiled when he saw it and crooked a finger at me.

"Come closer, little Rose, and I shall tell you the secret of that blade."

"No, thanks." I shook my head as I scrambled another step back, tucking the news that the blade had a history away for a chat with Irene later. "I'm not really interested in sharing any family secrets. And besides, it's time for you to leave this place."

With the smile still on his face he rushed me. Blind luck showed me an opening. I slipped closer than I was comfortable with, letting my blade thrust down through the enclosure of his hideous arms then up again. The magick was still with me for the blade never slowed, slicing through flesh clear to the bone as it went. It was the first blood he'd lost to me and from the look on his face, it shocked him. His surprise was my advantage and I took it, going for his throat like a cornered rat. Screw dignity, I'm all about survival.

I'd managed another couple of good blows before he recovered. Once he was back on his feet, my offense went back to defense. The grin on his ruined face took on a macabre image as he licked his lips.

"Ah, I smell it again. Fear adds to the taste of prey."

Okay, that went beyond creepy. He bared his teeth at me as if he knew exactly what image was playing through my mind. There wasn't anything in the scroll about being eaten. Of course, there wasn't anything in the scroll period about what happened if I failed. Michael probably didn't want too many details in the job description. That could put the recruitment numbers into the toilet.

Thinking of Michael had me wondering what the hell he thought I had going for me that he would have left the cup around. Surely it wasn't to embarrass him on my first round.

Remember who you are, Rose.

The echo of my grandmother's voice only seemed to add to the rush of noise around me. I tried to concentrate, but it wasn't easy since I was trying harder not to get killed. Why would she want me to remember who I was? I'd barely gotten used to who I apparently was, and it wasn't turning out to be enough to keep me from getting my ass kicked all over my supposedly sacred cavern.

Remember what you've always been. Stop looking at what you think is and remember what the magick inside you is like, what your magick has always consisted of.

That wasn't any more helpful. Unless…my brain finally found its connection to my heart and that kickstarted my thought processes. An idea bloomed into being. There were a lot of things I didn't know about me, but I did know that I was and always had been an elemental witch. Working with the elements was my strong point and the spells I used that connected with their power were my most effective ones. I felt myself panting for breath, and now that brought a smile to my face as I felt the air moving in and out of my lungs.

Taking a deep breath as I rose to my feet, I exhaled as Monster Man came at me again. As I exhaled, I connected my thoughts with the sylphs of the Air. I could almost hear them giggle as they took the breath I offered and turned it into a gale wind that threw him back against the stone walls with a disgusting crunching sound.

It was temporary, I knew. I couldn't stir up a hurricane inside the cavern, not without blowing myself against the stone right along with him. The wind would only keep him distracted for a short time, but I was beginning to feel myself center again. This was the kind of magick I understood. I just had to keep moving in this direction somehow. Then I spotted them scurrying back among the fallen rocks around the pool. Salamanders. Fire elementals.

I reached out to them just as Mr. Creepy stood and started for me again. Sidestepping his next onslaught without an inch to spare, I rolled over to the pool and cast my thoughts to the little critters. This time, though, I didn't want to play. I needed to end this fight, and I needed to end it now. I was in no shape to do more than run away, and sooner or later, most likely sooner, I would be out of energy to run with.

Maybe it came from hanging out in the cavern, maybe I had just never needed that kind of energy, but the closer I got to the salamanders the more I could feel the fire inside them. They held a heat and a passion I'd never found in them before. For such tiny creatures, I sensed a raging inferno inside their bodies. That inferno flamed up through their eyes as I called out for it and to my surprise the fire jumped to me. Its presence filled me with energy and with a rage that consumed everything that distracted from my focus on the moment. Using it as fuel to build the fire, I began to gather my will. The flames bloomed into a torrent inside me. I knew I could focus it, knew I could send it where I wanted, where I needed it to go. And I knew it would do what I needed it to.

I turned as he rushed me again. Power flooded out of me, and in front of my eyes, the salamanders grew to the size of small dragons. They circled around behind me like a line of precision flamethrowers. As I let out my cry and released the inferno inside me, fire shot out of them as well, red and hot and destructive. Our spell caught the demon dead center.

He stumbled, stopped to stare at us for a moment. His mouth opened and closed but no words came out. That alone was a victory, I thought. Then his fingers fumbled down to his waist, scratching along his belly as if to fling off the red hot fire. A hole appeared where the flames had landed, growing until the center of him looked like a macabre chiminea. He staggered, blood seeping from the corner of his mouth as his hands batted at the growing flames licking their way up his body. His lips tried to form words. All that came out was a scraping sound that shook the rocks around me.

In spite of the fire and the blood, he still didn't drop. His faculties had to be impaired though, for I'd worked us around to where he stood in front of the pool. He'd never taken his eyes off me, just followed me around until his back lined up with the pristine water.

In spite of the impact of my blows, I wasn't quite ready to jump and shout yet. I've seen enough horror movies to be wary of the monster that rises from his supposed death to kill again. That was a mistake I wasn't going to make. I called the wind once more, sending out my breath before he gathered the energy to rush me again. It hit him full force, slamming him back against the edge of the pool.

For a moment I thought it was done, that he would fall through the portal and be gone. Instead, he lifted himself, caught half in and half out of the portal. It was an eerie sight as I could only see the half that remained out of the portal, like the other half had been wiped away. He gave me a tiny nod then looked down at his burning belly. The gesture should have made me wary. My only excuse was I couldn't take my eyes off the fire consuming him. His hands dipped down into it, caressed the flames coating his fingers in a weird pseudo-sexual way that made me more than a little nauseous.

"Thank you for the gift, little ShadowWalker. I shall keep your tastes in mind for when I return."

Before I could blink, fire rushed out at me, the flames consuming everything between me and the pool. Searing heat blasted me off my feet. I caught a glimpse of him tumbling back into the water before the world around me faded to black.

Chapter Nineteen

I woke up disoriented, darkness all around me and the putrid odor of rotting things making me gag. My skin felt stretched tight from the fire in the cavern, but I felt no blisters, no skin peeling off. That could only be a good thing. Granted, it was hard to tell in the dim space, but I appeared to be more traumatized than damaged. Sometime later, I would ponder whether it was luck or something else. Super power healing would be a nice touch. I ached all over, though, so I wasn't sure about the super healing part. The smallest movement sent pain throbbing through my muscles. My body didn't seem happy with my new job.

"What the…where…how…"

I knew I sounded incoherent but it went right along with how I felt, so that was no big surprise.

Talk about your paradigm shift, I thought. The cavern was gone. What surrounded me was no longer dirt, stone and fire. Though I couldn't tell for sure, it appeared to be concrete, mud and garbage. Beat-up boxes, broken bottles and assorted types of disgusting trash lay in piles all over the room. My stomach heaved in rebellion. My head felt fuzzy, and though the room wasn't exactly spinning, it wasn't level and normal either. The lingering effects of my ShadowWalking made it hard to concentrate on the here and now. I'd have to get used to it if I was going to be so rudely thrust from one world into the next. I sniffed, not the smartest move I could have made, but my senses were picking up an odor beyond the rotting piles of garbage. Thanks to the garbage, though, it was hard to tell what it was. Trying to sit up had me painfully aware of why I was so disoriented.

"Ow!" My fingers probed the egg-sized lump on the back of my head.

"I think it was the third time he hit you that raised most of that."

Matthias' dry voice, so close behind, me made me jump, a movement that didn't help my head at all.

"Easy," he warned. "I don't think there's much room to move around in here."

"Then stop scaring me to death." I touched the lump again. "The third time?" My voice sounded dry and scratchy. I smelled a hint of smoke on my clothes, which added an unpleasant sensation to my already roiling stomach.

Matthias nodded. "You came to swinging. From the looks of things, I'd guess you'd been fighting already so when they tried to grab you, instinct took over. You actually did pretty good, knocked one of them on his ass before his buddy cold cocked you."

"I don't know that it was instinct as much as fear."

He looked me up and down, squinting in the dim light. "Tough ceremony, huh?"

"Tough doesn't begin to describe it. If we live through this, have I got a story to tell you."

"I'm going to take it that your decision got made in the affirmative and the world is now safe for democracy."

I nodded. "Not that it seems to have done a lot of

good so far, but yes was my answer. Democracy might be okay, but the rest of the important stuff is still at risk. No one appears very impressed with my new status."

"Not true. I was very impressed watching you kick those guys' asses. You didn't even hesitate."

"Fear will do that to you. That and the fact they were about half the size of what I was fighting before I landed back home."

"Half the size, huh? Should've been a piece of cake for you, then."

"Speaking of cake, I want one."

Matthias glanced around. "Sorry, no can do at this point."

"Not now. When we're done with this. Again, provided we live through it."

"Okay. Umm, now that you've got the super powers going, I'm leaving the planning up to you."

"That would be a very large mistake on your part. I thought we discussed my lack in the planning department earlier." I looked around me and shook my head. "And dumb luck doesn't seem to be working out very well. I don't even want to know what that smell is."

"You're right, you don't."

Matthias shifted a bit to make some room next to him. I scooted over beside him before thinking to check what was under me. Something squished beneath my butt, and I had to swallow hard. My head wasn't clear yet, but my stomach had slowed to a now and then rotation that gave me hope I wasn't going to add another smell to the horrific potpourri already filling the place. I glanced up at Matthias, who looked like he'd had almost as long a night as I had.

"Well now that we have my future celebration planned out, let's get back to the present. What the hell happened? And where the hell are we?"

"You're not going to like the answer to either one of those questions."

"Boy, is that not a surprise."

Matthias sighed. "Once you'd headed to your ceremony, Eddie and I went back to your house. Irene told us it might be a while and that you would likely return to your house rather than hers when you were…done."

I glanced around. "Okay, here's a news flash. This isn't my house."

Matthias snorted. "No shit. We got as far as the front yard before they jumped us."

"Vigil?" I started to ask if Yvette was there as well, but he shook his head.

"Espinosa."

"We're with Espinosa?"

He nodded. "Might have gotten the drop on them too, if you hadn't shown up."

I raised a brow. "I was wondering how I got there."

"I take it you didn't know you were coming home."

"I didn't know I'd be alive to go anywhere. Last thing I remember, my future looked like it was pretty much toast. Literally. So I just showed up?"

"Yeah. One minute it was just us in the yard, the next you were laying there by the front door. It was enough of a distraction for me to lose my focus. And that lost us the ballgame."

"Don't feel alone with that. It's been that kind of night for me, too. I'm beginning to believe it's the theme for this whole new life I've got. At least they didn't tie us up."

"Makes you wonder why they didn't think they needed to."

Damn, I hadn't thought of that. "Maybe they just forgot. Or they figured the smell in here would immobilize us."

I got to my feet and felt my way to the painted window, trying not to guess what any unidentified things I touched might be.

"Maybe." Matthias frowned. "But it kind of worries me. Vigil would have come at us with more magick, less brute force. I thought having it be Espinosa kind of gave us an advantage."

"Really?" I looked at him like he was crazy. "I got another news flash for you. We don't look like we're at any advantage in this situation."

"No, that thought didn't last very long. Things changed."

I rolled my eyes. "Again, not a surprise."

"Part of what changed has to do with…our motivation."

"Our what? Has he got an army out there?"

"No. Right now the men he's got aren't our biggest worry."

"They aren't?" I really didn't like the sound of that.

"There are other things he's got that sort of…give us a reason to be more cooperative."

"What sort of things?" My dislike was growing into a really bad feeling. Or maybe it had mixed with the bad feeling I'd had for the last several hours. Or maybe this was the only kind of feeling I was going to have anymore. I realized it could be any one of those choices.

"Rose," his hesitation let me know I so wasn't going to like what he had to say. "Espinosa has the cup."

"What! How is that possible? It was there, in the place with me."

"I don't know. Maybe there's some sort of…attachment it has to you, since it didn't get to leave when…"

"When it was supposed to."

He nodded. "It was lying right there beside you when you…arrived."

"So it's stuck to me. Even after I drank? That was the one thing I hoped would work out better."

"Like Irene told you, the cup has to be carried back by someone going back into the shadows. Usually it's the ShadowWalker who is passing on. But in your case…"

"Granny had to leave, and she couldn't take the cup because she hadn't passed it to me. Dammit, I was sure since it waited around for me to drink, it would have the courtesy to leave after I did."

"Well, I guess its manners aren't what you expected. And there's more."

"Just spit it out. I don't think I can be any worse off than I am now."

"Don't bet on it. Espinosa has Eddie."

I looked around, realizing I hadn't given Eddie a thought in all of this. Like I hoped I'd find him leaning up against a wall, picking at his scabs. I covered my face with my hands. What I really wanted to do was cry. A good cry would at least have been something useful for my emotions. But now didn't seem like an appropriate time, and I didn't think Matthias would have the patience for it. Besides, if I cried there was a chance I'd open my mouth, and if I did that the smell would get to me, and I'd puke. I'd avoided that scenario all this time, and I sure as hell didn't want to give into it now.

"Well, shit." I almost plopped down again before I remembered what was under me.

I wanted to go back to my safe little house and my safe little life. I wanted to crawl in my safe little bed and pull the covers over my uninformed head and let the world save itself. I thought about the cup, remembering the feel of it in my hands, remembered the faces and the voices. And I remembered their cries, their sadness.

"Sit down and focus for a minute, Rose. See if you can feel the cup, see where it is."

I looked around again. "I'll focus, but I'm not sitting down."

Matthias sighed. It was a sound I'd heard from him a lot in the short time we'd been together. I let out a sigh of my own as I sat down on what looked like the safest pile of shit. With my feet planted on the ground in front of me, I breathed in and out a few times, trying not to gag too hard. I focused my thoughts inside instead and to my surprise, the cup floated in front of me. The vision seemed so real I almost reached out to touch it before another hand grabbed it. Vigil's hand.

"Shit!"

Matthias frowned at me. "What?"

"The gang's all here."

Chapter Twenty

I didn't have a chance to explain to Matthias how our hand basket had drawn closer to Hell before the door slammed open and two thugs walked in. They were Espinosa's men. I could tell from the fact they were smiling as they entered and stuck a gun in our faces. Tony only hired men who enjoyed their work. One of them looked over at Matthias and wiggled his gun a bit. Guess it's a guy thing.

"Time to go, asshole. You and the pretty lady get to join the party now."

"Yeah." Thug Number Two snorted. "You're the scheduled entertainment."

Tony didn't hire them for their wit.

Matthias rose to his feet, and both men snarled as he did. Their guns wobbled and waved along with their hands, and I worried they were going to shoot him right then and there.

"Make it slow and easy." Thug Number One waved the gun closer to Matthias. "It'd be just as cool with me to take you in there dead instead of alive. You ain't the one he wants."

Thug Number Two grinned. I was sure I wasn't going to like what came out of his mouth next. My skills of perception were getting pretty sharp.

"Or we could rough him up a little before we go in. That'd be pretty entertaining."

More snorts of amusement followed this proposal. I wondered if their bravado had its roots in the bruises I saw on them and the blood I'd seen on Matthias. Guess the confrontation had been sort of a draw, and they weren't willing to lose the upper hand this time. No tough guy likes to look bad even if it's in front of the person they plan to kill.

"Nah." Thug Number Two chimed in. "Tony's waiting, and he don't like to wait." He glared at Matthias, who gave him a blank stare. "But once they stop talking we're going to find us a little corner. Then it's time for some payback."

He looked over at his buddy, and for a minute, I thought they were going to high-five each other. Matthias rolled his eyes as Thug Number One shoved him toward the door.

Thug Number Two jerked me from the floor and herded me out the doorway behind the others. As I tripped over some unidentifiable object, feeling every bump and bruise the fight with the demon had left me with, I found their excitement more than a little annoying. I also found it more than a little annoying that I couldn't summon up my super powers. What was the use of having them if they weren't available 24/7, I thought. I hadn't gotten even five minutes to enjoy my victory over Monster Man either. No cake, no balloons, not even a pause in the endless flow of people and things trying to kill me. If they ever gave me the chance to write a line in that scroll for my future replacements, I was going to mention the complete lack of celebratory events that awaited them. In my opinion, that's something they should know before they make their decision.

We were ushered into a big open warehouse. Well, shoved is more the appropriate word. Thugs One and Two took a great deal of pleasure in almost pushing Matthias to the floor. He turned on them when they did, and they backed up a step before recovering their machismo. They did the smartest thing to stop him, which was to shove a gun in my face. This made my estimation of their intellect go up a bit. Maybe pain is a good teacher.

"Frankie!"

Espinosa's shout got the gun out of my face.

"Quit messing around and get 'em over here!"

Able to breathe again once the weapon of my destruction left my face, I took a look around. The place was in a state of abandon with a thick carpet of dirt and other assorted objects on the floor and every other window broken out. The only thing missing were the pigeons, although there was evidence that they visited now and then. Guess Espinosa's thugs scared them away with their charming dispositions. Probably tried to shoot a few of them for practice. Or for dinner.

One glance told me we were in serious trouble. Vigil stood in the center of the mess, Espinosa on one side and Eddie on the other. Eddie wasn't looking too good either. The long day had taken a toll on all of us, but I had hope Matthias and I would make it out of this. My boundless optimism again, I guess. From the looks of him, Eddie's time was almost up, though.

Vigil held the cup in his hand. I almost dropped to my knees as the sound of the wailing from it slammed into my ears. Guess it was a subtle reminder that the job wasn't finished. And that the little good I'd done so far was in jeopardy of being reversed. In umbra, vires. I whispered the words, hoping the strength showed up wherever I needed it to and not just beside the spring. If my super powers were location-centered, I was in deep trouble.

I actually got a straight answer to a question this time. It did. I felt the strength of cold steel flood my spirit as soon as the words left my lips. My knees straightened, and I met Vigil's smug look head-on. Something in my gaze must have shown a change for his smug factor dropped just a bit, and he looked away.

Beside him, Eddie seemed oblivious to our entrance, but Espinosa never took his eyes off us. Not until he turned to Vigil and smiled. It was no prettier a sight than Eddie's face had become for it held death in it too. That look told me Tony had no intention of letting us walk out of here. Things were deteriorating all around us it seemed.

"We meet again, Mrs. DeSalvo."

Vigil's voice echoed in the empty space. I searched inside me for a way to wipe the smugness off his face completely. I smiled back at him.

"Not quite under the same circumstances, though."

"Yes. Yvette informed me of your elevation in rank." He smirked as he lifted the cup up for me to see. "Things do change, don't they? They change all the time."

"You got your merchandise, Vigil."

Espinosa shifted uncomfortably beside him. Tony was a businessman at heart. Chitchat wasn't part of the deal. As far as he was concerned, this deal was done.

"Let's wrap this up and get out of here."

"Our business is concluded when I say so, Mr. Espinosa."

The mask dropped off Vigil's face again, and even a mundane player like Tony could feel the difference. If I'd been Tony, I'd have taken a step back. Hell, I'd have run out of the building shooting as I went. I didn't think he would appreciate my input though, so I kept the thought to myself. Besides, if the red growing on Espinosa's face was any indication, he wouldn't have stepped back anyway. He was used to being feared, or at the very least spoken to in a respectful manner. The rules of the game had changed, but it looked like no one had told him.

"I've acquired the item you wished for and the person you wished for. Our business is done."

He threw the words at Vigil like a dare. I couldn't help but credit him with bravery. Could have been stupidity, but I like to think the best of people when we first meet. My opinion changed when I saw Yvette move up behind him. He turned as she wrapped one arm around his neck. He struggled for a moment, confusion covering his face. But he was in no way prepared for the situation he'd gotten himself into.

Yvette bent toward his neck, a smile on her face that sent shivers down my spine. It must have done the same to Espinosa for his struggling became more frantic. Yvette wrapped the other arm around him and he stilled, a look of absolute horror etched on his face. Although his mouth moved, no sound came out as she latched on to him with those ruby red lips. Horrifying sucking sounds would have covered any protests he made anyway.

The worst part for me was I could hear Espinosa's life force being drained, could hear the sound of his soul being eaten. I wanted to put my hands over my ears, but I found I couldn't look away. The voice inside me told me it wasn't my job to look away. There wasn't anything I could do for Espinosa either, except watch him die. That, and promise myself Yvette was toast.

I couldn't imagine the thoughts going through Espinosa's head, but at least one of them had to be kicking himself for not investing in better security. His back-up left a whole lot to be desired. While Yvette was giving their boss the Hug-O-Death, Thug One and Thug Two gaped at the scene. I could see the gears in their heads struggling to turn. The looks on their faces showed exactly when the news that the game had changed caught up with their brains. Confusion gave way to horror as Espinosa's body grew limp. Yvette dropped her love grip, and Espinosa sank to the floor like an empty sack. But then maybe I was wrong about their brain capacity. All it took was Yvette taking one step toward them as she licked Espinosa's blood off her lips. They didn't even look at each other, just took off in opposite directions. Yvette laughed as she stepped over what was left of Espinosa to stand by Vigil. He gave her a smile. What he needed to do was offer her a handkerchief. The blood was starting to drip down her chin. Beside her Eddie grunted, his gaze locked on the red liquid oozing out of her mouth. I couldn't tell if he was fascinated in a good way or horrified in a bad way. Either way he couldn't take his eyes off her. That couldn't be a good thing.

"Now, Mr. Espinosa, our business is concluded." Vigil didn't even spare the man at his feet a glance. His gaze was all on me. "Since Mr. Espinosa has been taken care of, you and I can finish our business as well, Mrs. DeSalvo."

"You know, Vigil, I have to say I'm not impressed with your managerial techniques. They don't bode well for your business sense."

He raised a brow. "Really? And why is that, dear Rose?"

"Business is about negotiating. I don't think Mr. Espinosa would be enamored of your negotiating skills."

Beside me, Matthias sucked in a breath. Guess he wasn't enamored of mine either. I glanced over at him, and noticed he was frowning down at the ground in front of Vigil then looking over at Eddie. Eddie must have lost his fascination with Yvette because now he stared at the cup. Vigil noticed his gaze and handed it to him, smiling like a benevolent grandfather letting the small child play with an expensive toy. Eddie continued to stare at it, turning it over and over in his hands. As Matthias looked over at him, Eddie looked up and their gazes locked. Something passed between them for Eddie gave a small nod. Beside me Matthias let out a breath. I didn't have time to figure it out, and I could only hope it was something good. We were in desperate need of something good. With that hope in mind, I turned my attention back to Vigil.

"I don't think I'm interested in being your business partner now, Vigil. Partnerships don't seem to be something you're good at."

"And are you a good businesswoman, Mrs. DeSalvo?"

"Nope. But then I never claimed to be. Besides, you know that legacy thing of mine you talked about? It didn't turn out to be quite what you told me. Now, I don't want to call you a liar to your face. That would be rude. But it just doesn't seem like you were being completely honest and up front with me. The lack of those qualities doesn't bode well for a potential partner."

"But, my dear, how do you know for sure my words were the lie? Perhaps the ones who told you something different were the ones not being honest."

"Experience. It all boils down to that. My experience with you has really not been a good one. Again, not meaning to be rude, but your actions have sort of fucked up my life. Attempting to frame me for Eddie's murder, deceiving me about your relationship with my grandmother, those weren't nice things to do to me."

"I am inexperienced as a mentor. Perhaps my methods were a bit too extreme. I had hoped the specter of Edward's death would motivate you to seek out the cup, an artifact you've shown no inclination to pursue before now. You may not have enjoyed my method but—" He nodded toward Eddie. "—it produced the desired result."

"Actually what that took was the honest truth. Not a method you tried."

He shrugged. "And so far as your grandmother and my relationship are concerned, that truth was private so others may speculate, but they do not know for certain. Claire and I did have a very intimate partnership."

"One you violated. Right before you killed her."

"She proved to be more stubborn than I'd expected. Much as you did."

"That's proof right there you weren't intimate with her. Anyone who knew her at all would have known how she'd react to that idea. As for me, well, thanks to the little journey you put me on, I know exactly what I am. I also know exactly what you did. You're a bad investment all around, Armando."

"Is that right? I believe you will find that the job description you've read can change at a moment's notice. Your grandmother found that out the hard way."

I couldn't stop my hands from clenching into fists. What I would have preferred was to wrap them around the smug bastard's neck. But first things first. Behind him, Yvette chuckled. My supply of witty comebacks to Vigil seemed caught up in my temper, but Yvette was another matter. I smirked at her.

"Just FYI, Red, your brother won't be joining us. He decided the trip wasn't worth it after all so he decided not to hang around."

To my disappointment, Yvette shrugged. "There will be another time. Of course, you won't be around to see it, but, that's the way it goes." She nodded toward the cup in Eddie's hand. "We have what we need to ensure our success. Too bad you won't be here to watch it."

Okay, well that shot down my bluff. I looked from her to Eddie. He gave me a long look that had me wondering if his coherency was fading after all. His movements seemed slower, more stiff, and the small awareness he'd had before was gone from his eyes. Just as I realized that, though, he smiled at me. It was a real smile, too, like he had something up his sleeve, but I just might like it. I'd only seen that smile once or twice in the whole time I'd known him. Looking at it now almost threw me off my game. Vigil chuckled.

"Yes, Mrs. DeSalvo, your husband appears quite enamored of the cup. I suppose it is a bit on the cruel side to give it to him now, after its pursuit has already caused his death. But I believe he deserves to know what he was looking for, don't you?"

"Leave Eddie out of this. You've done enough to him. You have the cup so let him go."

"To wander about the county aimlessly, forlorn and looking for a place to call home? I think not, dear Rose. No, I believe Edward might be of some use to me even now."

"What?" I so didn't like the sound of that. "Eddie's dead. He's not useable in this condition. Another few hours and he won't even be coherent." I glanced over at Eddie, who frowned at me. "I'm sorry, Eddie. But this is the guy that took your life. He's the bad guy. You can't stay with him."

"I believe that decision is not yours to make. What I'm offering Edward is the opportunity to remain this side of the grave, a change in location I'm certain he would prefer. Of course, I could simply leave his body to be found along with yours. There are ways to make it look as if your murderous intentions got the better of you. Mr. DeSalvo fought back bravely but alas, both of you were the victims of your desire for revenge."

The sickly sweet tone of Vigil's voice told me he was having far too much fun playing with me. I wanted him angry because anger made mistakes, anger made him distracted. Distracted, I just might stand a chance at throwing Vigil off his game. Luck was my new best friend.

"But enough of this chitchat." Vigil smiled at me. "It is time to end this. Since it is clear to me you suffer from the same inordinate amount of principle which plagued your grandmother, I realize that further persuasion would be useless. She, too, was unable to see beyond her own rather rigid moral code. Claire preferred to submit her power to another authority, a mistake I refused to make any more. It made her weak. It left her vulnerable." His gaze held mine as the venom inside him poured out. "It made her death almost easy."

It was hard, but I swallowed back the temper that rose in me with the promise that its time would come soon. I met Vigil's gaze, venom for venom, something it was clear he didn't expect. Maybe not knowing about the cup for so long had made me give it less presence than he did. He might have it now, but something told me if Michael could make it wait for me to learn then chances were an archangel could figure out who to send after it if his plans for me didn't work out. Always thinking, those celestial beings.

"And drawing your power from a monster makes you strong? Maybe my grandmother's choice didn't make her weak. Maybe it made her smart."

"Smart but dead? Not an acceptable end in my opinion."

"We all die, Vigil. All of us. Immortality is for the beings that use us. No matter how much power you think you have, you aren't getting out of this life alive, especially not with the choice you're making now. Do you honestly believe that putting yourself in the hands of a being that thinks of you as less than they are doesn't make you vulnerable? You're a fool, Vigil."

I spit the words at him, letting a little of my temper show. It must have been more than I thought for Yvette moved closer beside him.

"You gave up the best thing you had going to play with the bad guys." I felt the super powers juice up as I shifted my gaze to Yvette. "And you're stupid too. You think because the monsters are dressed up in pretty outfits and high heels that they're like you. You're even under the delusion you have some control over them. That kind of arrogance is a stupid man's trap. And it's going to be your undoing."

Deciding offensive maneuvers were in order, frankly because I was sick of being on the defensive and it just wasn't working out for me anyway, I took a step toward Vigil. As soon as I did, I felt energy radiating up from the ground in small but noticeable waves. There was something more to this space than an empty building.

The thought made me wonder what had taken place here. How many times had Espinosa used this spot for business, I wondered, and could that leftover energy stay in the walls, in the floor. I reached out to it and felt blood, death. A whole lot of bad energy washed over me, sliming me with its taint. The part that worried me was it felt familiar. Or there was something within it that felt familiar, a connection I couldn't quite identify. It didn't seem like the time to sniff the air again. There was no telling what I might inhale out here. Hantavirus, or something worse. Instead, I let myself relax, no mean feat considering the situation. Matthias moved up behind me. We were both probably going to die, but it was nice to have somebody standing on my side. I felt a bit stronger when I turned back to Vigil.

"You know, Vigil, Yvette and I had this little chat not long ago." I shook my head. "I told Yvette her little act with you was hard to believe. I mean, no being with such great power would let themselves be ordered around by some human, even if he was a big, bad

Weaver. Yet here she is, running your show, playing your moves like she's the one who choreographed them." I looked down at Espinosa's body, or what was left of it. "And cleaning up your messes. Does eating Espinosa make her the kitchen help? Whatever. Bottom line is, from what I can see, one of you just isn't as big and bad as you've been saying."

Vigil's face got red. "Shut up!" The mask was completely off now. "You bore me. Just because you took a sip from the cup you think it's made a difference in the balance of power. Nothing has changed. You can think you're big and bad all you want, but you're nothing now. We have the cup. You're finished before you even got started. Taking you out will be even easier than pushing Claire down those stairs." He smiled, and it was a sick look. "The power is mine. This place—" He waved his hands around. "—is mine. And your precious portal will be mine as well. No one will ever interfere with me again."

As he spoke, I watched Yvette's face. Disdain, and an evil Vigil appeared not to see, covered her pretty face. He was a fool to believe he wielded any power of his own, and now I understood that. The cup would never be in his hands. I didn't know exactly how, but I knew now he was stoppable. Yvette might even stop him for me, if I got lucky. Since I hadn't gotten lucky at all through this whole mess, I wasn't holding my breath for that. Before I could act on that newfound knowledge, though, Matthias spoke.

"Eddie."

His voice was firm and strong, with that quality to it that I knew held much of his magick. I felt power rising all around me, and I knew it wasn't mine.

"It's time." Matthias nodded at him. Eddie returned the nod.

"Enough!" Vigil's voice boomed in the empty space. "I don't know what foolish idea you have in your head, Mr. Romero, but your part in this little drama is over. I should never have allowed you to walk out of my house that first night. You and your insignificant pack of *elders* are no longer relevant. This place is mine, and their foolish rules have no bearing on anything anymore. It's time, all right, time to conclude this."

Vigil had been so focused on Matthias and his own rage he failed to notice Eddie, who was stumbling toward Matthias, the cup firmly in hand. As Eddie shuffled past him, Yvette let out a shriek.

"Don't let him go!"

She started for Eddie, and I moved in front of her. I wasn't quite sure what was going on, but I had an inkling. Behind me, Matthias had begun to chant, the power growing around him. Yvette's face twisted with rage as she tried to rake my face with her nails. I leaned back, sticking out one foot to trip her. Momentum worked on my side. She landed on her ass in a pile of pigeon poop. I *tsked* at her.

"Okay, that's girly fighting. I got better out of your brother."

She rose, growling, and I balled up a fist and punched her as hard as I could in the face. It rocked her head back a half inch or so. Not a promising start. She yelled back at Vigil even as her own fist swept toward my face.

"Stop him!"

Understanding finally dawned on Vigil's face, but

it came too late. I struggled with Yvette, thankful yet again for the superpowers because she'd have slid me aside in a second without them. The woman was freaking strong and pissed. I think the pissed helped with the strength because the more she yelled at Vigil, the harder it got to hold her. It might also have helped that she wasn't really giving the fight her full attention. She watched Eddie as he entered the circle Matthias had cast on the fly.

"No!" Vigil lifted his hands, and I felt the magick gather around him. "You cannot take this from me!"

The words formed themselves inside my brain, unlocking the thought that had been rattling around in there. My conversation with Irene came back to me, enough for me to remember her saying what had been woven could be unraveled. I opened my Sight and took a good look at Vigil. Seeing him through my inner eye, I saw all the wards around him. He was one paranoid guy. The energy weavings that covered his whole body in black, slimy strings were things of darkness, magick of a kind I had never done. For a moment I hesitated before Irene's words rose again. I didn't have to understand Vigil's magick, I just had to undo it. And that only took pulling the right string. I reached through the black tangle, but before my fingers could grip it, Yvette hit me with a force more like her brother's.

I hit the ground hard, my head bouncing a couple of times off the concrete floor. I might have seen stars, but before I could look up Yvette was on me, tearing at my hair, my eyes, my throat. She gouged her way toward my heart, intent on pulling it right out of my chest when I grabbed her hands and rolled over. With effort, I pressed her down to the floor beneath me.

Grossing her out clearly wasn't going to stop her.

It was hard to keep my focus on everything going on around me. Yvette's fists took first priority, but I didn't want anything else to sneak up on me unaware. Out of the corner of my eye, I saw the ground open in front of Matthias and my jaw dropped. Instinct at last connected the dots for me as the realization hit that this was where Eddie had lost his life. After the longest day and night of my life, I'd finally stumbled across the place I'd needed to find since I'd dug Eddie out of my rose bed. The sight of him stumbling toward the spot had a hard fist of emotion clenching my heart. Eddie walked straight toward the gaping hole, the cup tight in his hand. As he reached the edge, he turned to give me a sad smile before his feet sank into the ground beneath the concrete.

Vigil screamed, a sound that echoed around the emptiness. He'd been running when the ground opened up, and now he scrambled to stop before the hole swallowed him as well. For a moment he teetered on the edge of the open grave. I took that moment to find the string once more. Shoving Yvette back, I pulled on it as hard as the magick would let me, praying it would be enough.

Vigil's eyes widened as his feet slipped over the edge of the gaping hole. He flailed around for something to hold on to, bumping Eddie in the process. With a grunt, Eddie turned and gripped Vigil by the front of his shirt. I pulled harder on the string, unplugging the net of power and protection he'd woven around himself while Eddie pulled at his physical body. Vigil's eyes opened wide as saucers, his whole body swaying in a frantic dance to escape. The power wavered for a moment, rallying as Yvette struck back at me. I gave her another punch. Then I felt the magick surge again. When I looked over, Matthias had made another cut in his arm, the blood dripping from it, amping up the power radiating out from him. Vigil looked at me, hate in a purer form than I'd ever seen it glinting out of his eyes. His mouth opened in a wordless scream as he slipped below the yawning ground to tumble on top of Eddie before the loose coating of broken concrete sifted over them both.

Yvette screeched bloody murder, and I grabbed her hands as they went for my throat. I gripped them as I pushed her up and back, rising to my feet with a smile on my face.

"Time to go home, bitch."

I heaved her back, happy to see her roll a couple of times before she stopped. She steadied herself on her knees, growling at me. Panting, I stared across at her, feeling pretty damn good about myself. I just might live through this day yet. Of course, it would be easier if Yvette just disappeared. As she rose to her feet, I thought that might not be my luck. But she was hurt. I could tell that much by the stiff way she moved. Not down for the count but hurt. My boundless optimism reasserted itself as I spread my hands and grinned.

"Now your little toy's gone, Yvette."

She wiped her mouth with one hand, flicking the blood onto the ground. "There are others, ShadowWalker. I will find one, and it won't take me long. Humans are easy prey with their arrogance and their natural bend toward evil. A disgusting species, but—" She shrugged. "—they are what I have to work with."

"We'll see about that. For now, you're done here. Time to go." I waved my hand as if dismissing her. "Don't let the door hit you on the way out."

Her face twisted into an expression that didn't make it look its prettiest then she gave me the finger as she faded. In my head I heard a splash that did my heart good. One more monster back through the portal. All in a day's work, I guess, for a ShadowWalker. Feeling sort of proud of me, I couldn't wait to rub it into Jokyu's face.

I turned back to Matthias.

He looked a bit worse for wear. For some reason that only made him look hotter to me. Blood dripped from his arm to pool beside the broken concrete. His face was grim, and this time I knew the tattoo was moving beneath his skin. It made him look dangerous, but it also made my mouth water. Guess courting danger was still on my to do list, maybe permanently now. Another thing to ponder later.

"Well, that was fun."

I smiled over at him, and he laughed as he sat down. He shook his head when he looked up at me.

"I'm hoping the whole fight to the death thing doesn't add to your fee." I walked over to sit beside him.

"I'm already reevaluating the way I do business. Seems I need to include expenses along with my regular fee."

"Probably would be a good business move." I nodded. "Although I'm not sure how you'd come up with receipts for this one."

"Receipts? I thought you said you weren't a business woman."

"I'm all about the accounting from now on. My whole life has changed."

"I think that's probably an understatement."

"No shit, Sherlock. So it's receipts and not handwritten ones either."

"I'll see what I can do."

I nodded. For a minute we just sat there. Energy hummed around us although I felt more drained than I ever had in my life. And in a strange way, more satisfied. I knew a whole lot of things lay ahead of me I wasn't sure I understood, but I had survived the first day and that was something unexpected. Parts of me, hidden away for so long, thrummed under the surface, ready to be let loose. It would take me a while to explore them or to even realize they existed, and I could let them out of their cage now. I liked to think I'd be the one doing that and no more things would pop up unexpectedly, but I doubted that would be the case. I didn't quite know what I was going to do with my new life. Hell, I hadn't known what to do with the old one. But like it always did, change happened.

I smiled over at Matthias. "You know, I could start paying you by fixing you breakfast."

"Yeah, you could. Coffee, at least, would get you a discount."

"You're making it pretty easy on me."

"It's been a long day. I thought that was the least I could do."

"After we eat I should probably give Alexis a call. Catch her up on a few things."

He nodded. "She'll be glad to hear them. A whole lot of people are going to be glad to hear them."

"Yeah, I guess I'm going to have to find out some

names or get some introductions. Be nice to know who's on my side." I gave him a sideways glance which he ignored. "I'm thinking, though, I don't need to call Irene. Something tells me she knows everything that goes on."

"I got that impression, too. But it wouldn't hurt to reassure her."

"No, it wouldn't. I've still got some questions, and I'll stand a better chance of getting answers if I'm polite. At least that's what my mama always said."

Matthias stood and reached a hand to me. I let him pull me to my feet as I stared around at the mess the center of the warehouse had become.

"So," I looked at him. "Do we just walk out of here and go home or do we act like responsible citizens and phone this in?"

"I'm for the anonymous phone call. And not from your phone."

"Let's see, a grave with two dead bodies in it, both of whom clearly didn't die of natural causes, and the body of one of the biggest criminals in San Juan County with all the blood and other bodily fluids drained out of it. I'm thinking not even an anonymous phone call. I say we pack up and head to Mexico."

He smiled as he flicked something gross and sticky off my shoulder. "I don't think we need to leave town just yet. We didn't touch anything in the room or out here, at least not anything they could get fingerprints from. And with it being Tony Espinosa, I'm guessing they will write it off as a deal gone bad. Nothing connect us to it."

"So you hope."

"So I hope."

"Then what are we waiting for? Let's go put that coffee on."

Chapter Twenty-One

Matthias and I sat under the old elm in Greenwood Cemetery and watched the sun rise. I guess a necromancer has different ideas about what constitutes a hot date location. At least it had turned out to be a hot date. I hadn't known whether our meeting would be a date of any kind when I got his cryptic message. He asked me to meet him at Greenwood. He'd thrown in the word midnight after a long pause. One of these days I was going to have to teach the man how to talk on the phone in actual sentences.

There were other things nobody needed to teach the man. Sitting in a quiet cemetery making out probably wasn't everyone's cup of tea, but then they weren't kissing Matthias Romero. When it came to lip locks he was the master. With technique like his, I'd be a willing student anytime, anywhere, even a graveyard at midnight. Guess it was the necromancer's equivalent of the office supply closet.

"You look pretty in the moonlight."

"Wow." I stared up at him. "That's a sort of romantic statement. I didn't know you could do soft and gushy."

He grinned. "I figured you'd had a rough few days. I thought it might stress you less to say that instead of telling you I'm getting hard again looking at you lying there, naked in the moonlight with my scent all over you."

I slipped my hand down to cup the proof of what he said. Touching him left me feeling soft and gushy, so I decided to go with it. It was a good move on my part. I'd been right about him. He knew how to make sex worth the effort. Together we rode the passion we'd built until it took us both over the edge. Sated, at least for the moment, I stretched out on the soft grass, enjoying the thrumming of energy still moving through my body. The moon shone full overhead when I'd arrived, giving a silver glow to the old headstones. Now its outline was fading as the sun's rays started to make their appearance.

I glanced over at Matthias. He wore a self-satisfied smile. I had to admit he looked perfectly natural surrounded by the remnants of death, with the last of the moon's light shadowing his face.

"We might want to move. I'd hate to shock the early morning mourners."

He shook his head. "No one comes here this early."

I looked around me for my clothes. "You can't know that for sure. Some poor widow could show up with flowers any minute." I tossed his jeans at him. "We should put on clothes at least."

He shrugged the jeans aside and pulled me back down beside him. "In a minute. Rest, Rose. Just lie still and rest for a bit."

Since it sounded like a good idea, I snuggled back up against him. It surprised me he'd stuck around at all once things calmed down. Turned out we didn't even need to make the anonymous call. We drove to Matthias' house to clean up before he took me home. That was an interesting end to the weirdness. There were things in his house that made me wonder a whole lot about just who he was. But those questions could wait for another time.

As we walked in the door of my house, Mama told us that a sheriff's deputy had stopped by a half hour before, wanting to inform me of the death of my ex-husband. Mama put off the rest of his questions with wide-eyed innocence and a promise to have me call them as soon as I got home. Thankfully, Leon left for his barstool before the police came, so he wasn't there to add his input. If he had been, the sheriff might have waited around for me. Even after getting that news, Matthias stuck around. Having someone of the male persuasion in my life was going to take some getting used to, but then there were more than a few new things in my life that were going to take some getting used to.

There were things about having him with me that wouldn't take long, though. I stretched, enjoying the feel of my satisfied body. Matthias rolled to his feet, reaching for the jeans he'd flung down beside him. I tried not to sulk as he put them on.

"You were the one who wanted our clothes back on."

"Don't remind me."

He laughed as he reached a hand down to pull me up. "Come on, I'll buy you coffee."

"And breakfast?"

"You ask for a lot."

I frowned up at him. I'd finally found my underwear and sat down to put them on. Didn't want to leave any evidence behind. "You're the one who made me work up an appetite. Now you have to fix that."

He jerked me against him as I stood. "I'm good at

fixing things."

Yes, I thought, yes you are. If he kept kissing me we were going to be the sideshow for those sunrise mourners. It was hard, but I stepped back from him.

"Coffee. Breakfast. And talk."

"Ah, talk." He looked around for his shirt, which hung from a nearby bush. "I didn't think you'd let that one go."

"Nope. I want details, answers. Names."

His grin faded. "They want to talk to you."

I thought for a moment before shaking my head. "Not yet. I'm not…there yet. I've got a lot to process. And I have a feeling I'm going to have Jokyu breathing down my neck to come back to his torture chamber. For now, I want to know who. That's enough."

"They may show up on your doorstep anyway."

"No they won't, not if you tell them to back off for now."

"Alexis will want to talk to you. I can't stall her."

I blew out a breath. "I'll deal with her when she comes. You might warn her though that she'd better be more forthcoming than usual. I want answers."

"I can tell her."

****

The sunrise gave us a helluva show as we finished dressing. Shades of blue, gold and orange lit up the sky like dancers announcing the arrival of the Sun King. The sight buoyed my tired heart, even as it reminded me I had a world to save. Or at least my corner of it. I wondered how long I could wait before I had to get back to Jokyu and the training that would hopefully turn me into a halfway decent ShadowWalker. Hopefully I could take a minute to catch my breath, but

Yvette's parting words told me I'd better catch it quick. I glanced over at Matthias, a bit sorry to see he had all his clothes back on. I'd made a lot of mistakes in the past, especially in the area of the male half of the world. I had a lot of questions about who the man next to me was, and why he wanted to be a part of my life. Yeah, he'd stuck with me and that weighed heavily on the pro side. I was hoping the con side weighed a whole lot less.

It felt good to have someone next to me. The world might have changed in some good ways, too. Now I wasn't all alone in a game I didn't really know how to play. I gazed out at the wide sweep of green lawn to keep myself from dozing off.

"I think maybe I'll put up a remembrance marker for Eddie here. Although his mother will probably just take it down. Maybe I'll do something subtle, something she won't notice. It's really a beautiful place, even if it's full of dead people."

Matthias reached for my hand. "It's not only here for the dead, you know. Besides, the dead exist behind a thinner curtain than most people realize."

I nodded, surprised by the sudden lump blocking my throat. The image of Eddie's last smile floated in front of my eyes. In all the times I'd considered his demise, I hadn't thought of missing him. But I did. Matthias touched my face with his finger, wiping away the tear that had trailed down my cheek.

"He really did love you, in his own, strange sort of way."

"Yeah, I guess he did." And that thought still amazed me. I wondered how much difference it would've made to have known that while he was still living. It wouldn't have stopped the cheating, I knew, but it might have stopped so much of my anger and my sense of failure if I'd realized Eddie had real feelings for me.

"Don't second guess fate, Rose."

"How can you always tell what I'm thinking? I thought you could only hear the dead talking."

"Your face is an open book. I can hear you babbling inside your head just from the look on your face."

Matthias pulled me into his arms and held on tight. It felt good. After a moment he pulled back and cupped my face with his hands.

"You gave Eddie the chance to be noble, to be brave for you. You gave him the chance to end his time here with something positive to take with him. You can be proud of that, Rose."

"And of him."

Matthias nodded. "And of him."

"And now I have the chance to be noble, too."

He smiled. "You have the chance to be you now. To be who you've always been inside. You need to think of it that way. You need to believe in the magick that lives in you. It is yours, after all."

"To believe I'm a ShadowWalker. Like my grandmother. That's not going to be what's so hard to believe. After what I went through I can buy that. But buying the rest of it…I don't know. All my illusions are gone now, thanks to Yvette and her brother."

"Yvette and her brother?"

"When you know having an angel in your family tree doesn't automatically make you the good guy, you start to look at people differently."

"I can see where that would change things. It's going to be a lot of work, Rose. There are things you're only just now starting to understand."

"And things I have to let go of."

"Yes."

"You want to stick around for all that."

"I might. After all, you still haven't paid me."

"Uh-oh."

"Why uh-oh?"

"Well, you might be expecting more now that you know what I am."

"Rose, I always knew what you were."

"Yeah, and we're going to have a long talk about that. You and Alexis both held out on me, big time."

"Would you rather we'd pushed you into something you weren't ready to choose?"

"I'd rather you warned me about all of it, instead of leaving me to think I was crazy and deranged."

"From the short time I've known you I have to say don't let go of those thoughts yet. You just might be crazy and deranged."

I leaned back and punched him in the arm. He smiled.

"Don't knock it. From what I've seen, crazy and deranged could come in handy with the things you're going to have to do, Rose. And the things you're going to see. If you're already crazy and deranged, they can't drive you over the edge."

He looked down at me and the smile was gone. "People are going to think you really are crazy and deranged, you know that, don't you? People you care about."

I shrugged. "Not the ones I really care about. Well,

maybe Leon, but he's crazy and deranged too, so he can't really say much. The rest of my family, they already think that of me so it won't be a change."

"If that's the case, then things should go pretty smooth from here on out."

"You don't lie well, you know that? I know it won't be easy. I also know I could have lived my whole life never acknowledging any of this."

He nodded. "Yes, you could have. We're all very grateful you didn't."

"How do you know? Maybe the next person in line would be much better than me at all this."

"Maybe. I think there's an even better chance you're going to be really good at this."

He leaned down and kissed me before I could say anything else.

A word from the author…

I've been writing for as long as I can remember. Being a writer is more than something I do. It is the way I see the world, the way I process it. I believe in the power of stories. They make us smile, make us think and give us untold moments of enjoyment. My stories come from the landscape around me and the worlds I build in my head. I am proud to be a storyteller, and I hope my work leaves you both satisfied and entertained.

www.debradoggett.com

Thank you for purchasing
this publication of The Wild Rose Press, Inc.

If you enjoyed the story, we would appreciate your
letting others know by leaving a review.

For other wonderful stories,
please visit our on-line bookstore at
www.thewildrosepress.com.

For questions or more information
contact us at
info@thewildrosepress.com.

The Wild Rose Press, Inc.
www.thewildrosepress.com

Stay current with The Wild Rose Press, Inc.

Like us on Facebook

https://www.facebook.com/TheWildRosePress

And Follow us on Twitter
https://twitter.com/WildRosePress